Beatrice Ley

Fiesole

Volume II

Beatrice Ley

Fiesole
Volume II

ISBN/EAN: 9783337047313

Printed in Europe, USA, Canada, Australia, Japan

Cover: Foto ©Andreas Hilbeck / pixelio.de

More available books at **www.hansebooks.com**

FIESOLE.

A NOVEL.

BY

BEATRICE LEY,

AUTHOR OF "A GOLDEN MARY-BUD," ETC.

IN TWO VOLUMES.—VOLUME II.

LONDON :

BERNARD QUARITCH, 15 PICCADILLY.

1886.

LIST OF MISS BEATRICE LEY'S PRINTED WORKS.

POEMS 1866

PHŒNIX 1877

THE PILGRIM OF LOVE (in the *Daisy*) ... Nov. 1879

TRUE LOVE—JOHN PETERS 1881

GOLDEN MARY-BUD (in *Shorthand Magazine*) ... 1882

Ditto (as a Novel) 1883

EASTER FESTIVALS IN FLORENCE (in *Shorthand Magazine*) 1883

Ready for Press.

A COLLECTION OF SHORT TALES :—

    A NORTH COUNTRY LASS.

    I BEG YOUR PARDON.

    DIAMANTE.

    LA POVERETTÀ.

In Preparation.

A Novel in Three Volumes, called KEEPING STEP.

CONTENTS OF VOL. II.

ILLUSTRATIONS TO VOL. II.

FIESOLE.

CHAPTER I.

THE LOVERS' MEETING.

BERTOLDO and Alessio went together to the Lung-Arno della Zecca Vecchia on the following day, as they had appointed. They went after eleven, and found the lovers already there. They stood hand-in-hand with their backs towards the two spectators, who determined not to betray their presence unnecessarily. Pulling their hats over their eyes, they stole on quietly, until they were within hearing distance.

"My dearest Colomba, this is very provoking! It is three whole days since I have met thee—and now thou tellest me that I must see thee no more!"

"I do not believe that it matters to you!"

" Oh! beautiful angel, do not play with me.
Listen, I swear that I love thee alone!"

Bertoldo ground his teeth, but a warn-
ing pressure of Alessio's hand kept him
quiet.

" You say that you love me, but men—
ohimè! are such liars."

" Hast *thou* found it so ?　That gives me
surprise !　Who could tell aught to *thee*, but
the pure truth ?"

"I do not know !　But tell me, cannot
you live without seeing me ?"

" It is impossible !" he replied, melo-
dramatically.

" Poor thing !"

" But, Diavolo! Colomba, what is your
intention ?"

" To come no more."

" Hast thou no pity for me ?"

Colomba smiled; she had only been
playing with him from a desire to hear his
protestations—they had always been sweet
to her; but in her present frame of mind
they soothed her wounded vanity, and were
delightful.

" It is well ! If thou art good I may
come to thee sometimes in another place.

But I cannot come here; for they begin to suspect me, and I fear something might happen. There is no harm in our meeting sometimes to talk, therefore, I will still come; but not often. Art thou content?"

"I see that I must be content"—and he heaved a deep sigh.

"What is that ring on your finger?"

"Oh! it is only a little ruby!" And he held up his hand reluctantly.

"It is very pretty," said Colomba, taking it off and putting it on her own hand.

"Give it me back, bella; it is too large for thee. I will bring thee a far prettier one." His tone was so anxious that it aroused Colomba's suspicions, and she determined to tease him.

"I do not wish for another; I prefer this! Give it to me, Signore."

"I cannot! Anything but that."

"*This* is what I want—ah! I see well that you do not love me. All men are alike, 'twenty soldi for a franc!'"

The young man stood irresolute, not knowing what to do; but Colomba conquered; "I can say I lost it," he thought.

"Thou art mistress of all that belongs to me! keep the ring if it pleases thee. It is not pretty enough for thee; but thou wishest for it, therefore, it is thine."

Colomba smiled triumphantly, and twisted the ring round on her finger. To reward him for his docility, she said archly: "You will find me in the Cascine, at the second Piazza, the day after to-morrow. You can walk that way, if it pleases you, Signore."

"Certainly, I shall be there, my beauty."

"But now I must go, Signor Carlo. It is not fitting that I stay longer. Addio!"

"Arivederlà!"

She walked on a few steps, and then came back to him, her face bright with innocent mirth.

"Take it! there is your ring."

"But I gave it to thee."

"Did you think I would deprive you of it? You have looked serious ever since I took it. I know not who gave it to you; but it matters not, I have seen that you love me best." And, dropping the ring into his hand, she ran quickly away.

He stood still, looking after her.

"She is a good little thing," he murmured.

Soon after this, the gentleman walked away along the Lung-Arno. When he was out of hearing, but still in sight, Bertoldo exclaimed :

"Let me kill the thief, Alessio!"

"No, friend, we must act with prudence, and make no scandal. See you not, that our Colomba is a little flirt, but she is yet a child, and quite innocent."

"I could observe nothing but that brigand!"

"It may be that he is a brigand, but we must think first of Colomba. I wish to find out who he is, and then I will recount all to her relations, and they can guard her. Go to thy house quietly, and let me follow him. Thou art too angry to act with judgment; I will tell all to thee afterwards."

"I trust thee. Go, and good speed! But kill not the traitor, for I consider that to be *my* privilege!" And Bertoldo left Alessio, and walked hastily along the Viale.

Alessio followed the gentleman, keeping him well in sight—but he took care that he should not know that any one was following him.

Alessio particularly wished to find out who the young gentleman was, before they denounced him to anyone; for that ruby ring (which the gentleman had held out so that Alessio could see it perfectly) had put strange thoughts into his head. It was the exact counterpart of the ring he had sold to the English lady; and he felt sure that no other such ring existed in Florence. The design of the setting had been his own, and was as peculiar as it was handsome. Could this really be the same ring that beautiful creature had bought, with a blush of tender love? And was it to be thus lightly prized by the ungrateful rascal on whom she had bestowed it? Her pure and beautiful face arose before his mental vision, and he felt that he hated this man even more for *her* sake than for Colomba's. Had he not already discovered Colomba's real nature, this interview would have been as trying to him as it was to poor Bertoldo; but he had watched the lovers with the clear-sighted eyes of an indifferent spectator. Colomba was evidently not in love with this young gentleman, though her vain little head had been turned by his notice. She appeared to be enjoying a comparatively innocent flirtation—if such a thing can be termed *innocent*. Alessio thought that this trouble had been occasioned by his own fault; for he had let the girl go out alone, and that had led her into mischief. But she appeared to him not to be thinking of marrying this gentleman, but merely of wishing to be admired by him. Whatever his intentions were, he was sharp enough to understand what sort of girl he had to deal with, and he had evidently uttered no words but those of innocent admiration and vague protestation. He had been so careful not to frighten her that he had never attempted a caress. Poor Bertoldo's mad jealousy blinded him to the truth, but Alessio guessed all this. However, he saw that the love-making must be put a stop to at once. He would let no one have cause to make malicious insinuations against Colomba. And again, now that their engagement was broken off, she might begin to dream ambitious and impossible dreams of a gentleman-husband. It must all be put an end to as soon as possible. Poor silly little Colomba! He pitied her sincerely. But he almost smiled to himself at the thought of the way in which he had once idealized her, and how different was the real Colomba to what he had fancied her. He felt thankful that he had escaped that danger. And poor Bertoldo! *he* was not fancy free—and none knew yet how *his* troubles were to end.

All this time Alessio had been following the gentleman, and they had now reached the via Borgognissanti, where the young man entered a house. Alessio went up to it, and made a mental note of the number: Standing abstractedly before the door, he did not even see a gentleman who came out of the house, so impetuously that he almost knocked him down.

"Excuse me! A thousand pardons for being in your way"—said Alessio.

"I cannot believe my eyes! why, it is thou thyself, my Alessio," returned the gentleman.

"Ah! Signor Minuti, it rejoices me to see you! I did not at first recognise you."

"Nor did I recognise thee. What art thou doing there, standing like a statue? Surely, thou dost not find that house picturesque?"

"Oh, no!" and Alessio laughed—and then added: "I am in a perplexity, Signor Minuti, and perhaps you could give me help. May I tell you all my story—it is a long one?"

"Certainly, my son. Come with me to my studio." And the old man placed his arm in that of Alessio, and they walked together to the studio.

Something in the old man's kindly sympathy won Alessio's confidence, and he told him the whole history of his life, beginning with his love and his hopes, and ending with his disappointment. When he told of his discovery of Colomba's true nature, and of his consequent disillusion, and the breaking off of their engagement, Signor Minuti arose, and going up to him, clapped him cordially on the back, and shook him by both hands.

"My son, it is well, most well! I congratulate thee."

Alessio smiled. "It is not usual to congratulate a man on losing his betrothed."

"Ah, son, thou hast but lost a *woman*. Thou wilt now find thy *Art, she* will claim thee for her own!"

" Do you not believe in women, Signore ? "

" Not in such women ! She would have ruined thy career. There are some of another kind, angels of light, who spur men on to great deeds. *They* are not the rivals of Art, but her ministers. It may yet be your lot to find a Beatrice—a Laura."

"I hope so ! But I will not think of such things now. You have not yet heard all my story. Do I weary you ? "

" Oh no, not a bit ! Can you not see, imbecile ? " and the old man resumed his seat with a good-humoured laugh. He shewed great interest in the whole of Alessio's narrative, but when he told of Colomba's gentleman-lover, of the ruby ring, and of his remembrance of the English girl, then the old man's face grew very serious, and his manner became troubled.

" Ah ! Alessio mio, this is a bad world, a very bad world! But thou art a good fellow, so I will confide in thee, as thou hast confided in me. Know, that this devil *infernale*, whom thou hadst followed to the house where we met, is a certain Conte Carlo Bentivoglio ; he is a gambler and a roué, and as bad as can be imagined. But, by his deceptive gallantry, he has gained the heart of an angel, at whom he is unworthy even to look. She is a rich Inglese, evidently the same lady that you saw, for you have described her exactly. He loves her not for her beautiful soul, nor even for her beautiful face, but only for her money. Diavolo! think of that! an angel, a pearl, to be married for her money by such a rascal! And actually she has consented to marry him. She is so innocent, she cannot even believe in such wickedness as he commits. Ah! this world, this world! She is of age, therefore no one can prevent her from marrying him. Her parents are dead, and she lives with a silly, unsympathetic old aunt, whom she heeds not the least. Though thy disclosure will pain *her*, it delights *me*; for I hope it may be the means of awakening her from her delusion and saving her. As the little peasant girl is foolish and innocent there is nothing in this matter that we cannot bring before the young lady. I am sure her good heart will be full of indignation against the Conte for his wanton trifling with this child; for he might have ruined her good name. And the young lady's

jealousy and pride will be aroused when she
hears how *her* lover woos other women—and
would even have given away her present.
You must go and tell her all."

"Oh no! Signore, I pray you to do this
yourself! You are an old friend, and a
gentleman. How could I speak—to pain the
young lady!" and his face flushed.

"We will go together. For Miss Ina
Laurence knows I do not wish for her marriage; therefore, although she would hardly
doubt my word, I prefer to have a witness."

"But Colomba, what can be done for her?"

"I advise you to take her home to Fiesole
as soon as possible. You can tell her that
the gentleman is engaged to a young lady;
and I think that will put an end to the
romance in her quarter. No doubt she will
marry the young farmer, if he still cares to
have her. I daresay this shock will take all
the folly out of her."

Good Signor Minuti, how little he understood Colomba, — or Ina either, for that
matter! A woman's heart is a curious and
delicate thing, so mysterious in its workings
that it needs time and experience, even for a
woman to know her *own* heart.

CHAPTER II.

LIKE A QUEEN.

WHEN they reached the door of Ina's house, Signor Minuti looked at his companion, and was struck by the peculiarly woebegone and embarrassed expression on his face. A sudden compunction seized the good old man, and he perceived that it would not be fair, either towards Alessio or the young lady, to deal this blow so publicly. No! he would break the news first, and then call Alessio in as a witness. He sighed deeply; but he made up his mind to do his duty manfully.

"The Signora is not ready to receive," said the servant.

"It is the Signorina I wish to see."

"Enter then, Signore."

When they had reached the first floor

landing, Signor Minuti said to Alessio:—
"You wait there till I come for you. I will
speak with her first."

Alessio felt much relieved that the artist
had decided on this course of action. But
after he had seen his friend disappear into a
door-way, and the servant had run down
stairs, a sudden tremor came over him; and,
strong man though he was, he felt obliged to
seat himself upon a large wool-work divan
that stood in the middle of the entry. How
terrible it would be when Signor Minuti
called him to confront that beautiful young
lady, for him to tell her of her lover's perfidy.
That last word called up the thought of the
sorrow of which he was the unwilling messenger; and he forgot his own embarrass-
ment in sympathy for her and her pain. His
heart beat in responsive throbs of agony, the
echoes of what she must be suffering. Were
those beautiful tender eyes full of tears—was
she in a swoon? Ah! he wondered how she
was bearing her trouble. He sat there in
suspense, hearing nothing but the beating
of his own heart. At length a door behind
him opened—he started to his feet with a
blush upon his bronzed cheeks. He only

saw a comical-looking old lady, with a tumbled wig of hair, a striped dressing-gown, an extraordinary cap, and spectacles awry , on her nose.

"What want here ? " she said in bad Italian.

" I await the Signor Minuti," said Alessio, bowing politely.

" Oh, well ! " and she vanished again.

This episode seemed like comedy in the midst of tragedy, and only made the suspense more trying than before.

At last ! Yes, the door through which Signor Minuti had disappeared opened, and the painter came towards him. His face wore a puzzled expression ; but Alessio was too much agitated to notice that, or anything else—he merely followed mechanically.

When he entered the drawing-room he saw a sight he never forgot in all his after life. Standing by the window was Ina, her face rather pale, but apparently calm ; there was a questioning look in her tender hazel eyes, and she leant with one hand on the window-sill. A ray of sunlight fell upon her head like a golden glory—and to Alessio's poetic fancy she seemed more than a mere mortal creature. So calm, so unmoved, surely she was a very queen among women.

Signor Minuti could not understand Ina in the least. She had expressed no doubt as to the truth of what he had told her; she had merely listened passively. Was her calm the calmness of despair, or was she callous and heartless ? He looked at her doubtfully.

Not so Alessio ! he understood her better. He approached her timidly and reverently. She looked at him with no recognition in her gaze. How should she remember a common jeweller ! There was a questioning, wistful light in her eyes as she turned to him. She knew he was a jeweller, but she did not guess that he was the young genius the painter had praised so warmly the night before. She was trying to find out from his countenance whether she might believe his word. Something told her that she might trust him. Her quiet was not the quiet of despair or of heartlessness ; it was the calm of one who had received so sudden a shock that the mind was not yet able to realize it. What were vague, lover-like alarms, sad days passed in waiting, compared to such a certainty as this would be ? That her lover loved her not! She shivered slightly and clasped the window-sill tighter. Then, drawing herself up bravely, she said, in a sweet, low voice :

"Signor Minuti tells me that you have something to say to me. He told it to me himself, but I could not understand him very well. You will oblige me if you will tell it to me again—the whole truth, please!"

Alessio wished himself anywhere but where he was. He looked down at the carpet nervously, and his cheeks flushed a deeper red. Suddenly, he remembered what a mean scamp this lover of her's was, and how utterly unworthy of such a woman; so that to break off the marriage would be to save her from certain misery. This thought gave him courage, and he looked her in the face with the light of truth shining in his eyes. He would tell her all, for her own sake.

He repeated word for word what he had heard the Conte say to Colomba. When he mentioned the ring she gave a little cry and pressed her hand to her heart; her lips quivered ominously, and she turned her back upon them. Alessio continued speaking, telling her of how Colomba had returned the ring.

Then there was silence.

Ina did not cry, or scream, or faint. Her eyes were full of a supplicating agony, and her lips moved in silent prayer for strength. It was given. And, when she again turned her face towards the two men, they were awe-struck by her beautiful and wrapt expression. This was not what they had expected. That she suffered deeply was evident ; but she gave no sign. She was a brave woman—strong with a courage not of earth.

"Thank you for telling me the whole truth. This—this young girl is—is—what *is* she?"

"She is a naughty little flirt, though an innocent girl. She was engaged to Alessio here."

"Ah! I understand. So this has wrecked your life too. And she loved Carlo—Signor Bentivoglio—the most?" And Ina looked at Alessio with some pity, but also with an expression that seemed to say, that it was very natural any girl should like the Conte best.

"No, Signorina. I had myself broken

off our engagement yesterday morning ; for
I had already discovered that la Colomba did
not suit me. But she certainly must have
been flirting with the Conte whilst still engaged to me. As for loving, though !—why,
I do not believe she ever loved either of us."

" You do not understand," Ina said, decidedly. " You tell me she is young and
innocent, and—and—that—that he was
courting her ; how could she have helped
loving him ? It was not possible ! "

" But now it will all be at an end ; she will
go home, and he will not be able to harm
her," said Signor Minuti, consolingly.

" What are you saying ? Do you think
he would wish to harm her ! Do you
think I could feel happy if I knew that she
was breaking her heart for him, and he his
for her—and all because of me ! "

" Why, Ina, you are mad ! What do you
mean ? "

" This, Signor Minuti," and she spoke with
a sweet and simple dignity that was far more
touching than tears : " Conte Carlo Bentivoglio loved me once—yes, he loved me truly
then—and we became engaged. Afterwards
I noticed a change in him, but I did not then

know the reason.   Now I understand it all.
He had seen another, one whom he liked
better, and his love for me died, killed by
the power of this stronger passion.   Do you
think he would have forgotten his love for
the sake of a mere fancy?   That he would
neglect me to *flirt* with a peasant girl?   Ah,
no!   I know what the poor fellow must have
suffered.   Bound by honour, he could not
break his pledge to me, and he remained
true to it, although his heart was given to
another.   But they shall be united, and I
will no longer prove an obstacle to their
happiness."

"You little idiot! you little angel!"
exclaimed Signor Minuti, as he seized Ina's
hand enthusiastically.   His eyes were glistening with a suspicious moisture, and his voice
trembled as he spoke.   "Ah, Ina! this
comes of feeding the imagination on pure
romance and noble sentiment.   Why, child,
you know nothing of life.   Do you mean to
say, that you think Signor Bentivoglio would
marry a contadina?"

"If he loved her!"   Ina's eyes flashed
indignantly, and she drew away her hand
with the air of an offended queen.

Alessio felt that he could have fallen down at her feet, and have kissed the ground she stood upon. To think that so vile a rascal should have won a heart like this !

"But, I tell you, he would not marry her."

"You mean that their disparity of rank would be disagreeable to him ? I cannot think that you are right. But if you are, then it shall be *my* duty to show Signor Bentivoglio that true love is worth more than noble birth, and honour more than life."

"I think we had better leave you now. I am sorry, my dear, that we have been obliged to pain you."

"You could not help it ! Life is full of pain. It is always best to know the truth."

"Which you are very far from doing," thought the painter. "Alas ! poor child; the greatest shock yet awaits her when she learns a twentieth part of the meanness of the creature she has loved. Good-bye, Ina," he added aloud.

"Good-bye, Signore. And you, too, good-bye,—and thank you. I pity you, for you also must have suffered."

"Your servant, Signorina ! "

To the last she appeared brave and self-controlled; but when they had left her she flung herself down on her knees beside the sofa, and cried as though her heart would break. She felt that henceforth all the world would be a blank to her. She was still determined to do her deed of self-sacrifice, but she counted the cost. Ah! how fervently she prayed to God, with what yearning love her heart turned to that Father whose love o'ershadows us all. She felt that His was indeed a tender love that would never forsake her—and she said to herself that beautiful verse :—

> " He shall cover thee with His feathers,
> and under His wings shalt thou trust :
> His truth *shall be thy* shield and buckler."

And when she arose from her knees she was comforted.

" Ah! Signore, how I thank you for having taken me there. You have given me a memory I shall treasure all my life. It is an honour to have seen her—among women she is indeed the queen—a pearl without price! I said to her 'your servant, Signorina,' and those words of mere form came from my heart. What would I not give to be her servant,—to work, to fight, to *die* in her service! And I should feel myself but too well paid if she gave me only a smile."

"Take care, Alessio, that thou losest not thy heart." And Signor Minuti smiled.

"Oh, Signore, this is not a moment for such thoughts! And she is too far above me! A man may love an angel in Heaven, or a crowned queen—love, admire, revere. Those are my feelings for her. The mere idea of any other thought offends me."

The painter saw that the young man was telling him the exact truth. His poetic imagination and chivalrous feelings were fired with an innocent admiration, kindled by the vision of a surpassingly noble woman. It would be wronging his friend to try to bring his thoughts down from Heaven to Earth.

"And, Signore, you speak of my *losing my heart*. It seems to me, that if I fill it with *her* image, I should, in effect, *find* my heart. Filled by so sweet a dream, think how precious it would become! Why, the world already appears to me more beautiful."

" Thou hast reason on thy side, Alessio !
There lives not a more good and beautiful
creature. But, alas! she suffers."

"Not *alas*, Signore; for she has the
courage to endure. And it is the noblest
who are given the most to bear—because
they are so near to God that He can comfort
them. Yes! and He *will* comfort her."

CHAPTER III.

THE FALSE AND THE TRUE.

AFTER parting from Signor Minuti, Alessio entered his shop. He stood, silent and thoughtful, in the door-way that led into the house. He remembered that Colomba had appointed to meet her gentleman-lover on the day after the morrow, and, of course, this rendezvous must not be permitted. He also thought how disagreeable was his own position with regard to her— apparently her betrothed, in reality nothing of the kind. How much had happened on this most eventful day. He did not for a moment entertain such wildly Quixotic hopes as Ina Laurence; for he knew her lover's character better than she did. He trembled for her as he thought of the cruel awakening that awaited her. The more he thought, the more advisable it seemed to him, that he should tell Colomba the truth at once, and convey her home that same evening. She would be safest in her mother's keeping; for *he* had no authority over her now, if, indeed, he had ever really possessed any. It was their dinner hour, so he decided to let them eat in peace, and then afterwards break his tidings to Colomba. He did not fear for her heart—he knew that if she cared the least for any one, it was for Bertoldo.

Their dinner passed off quietly and un-eventfully; la Fortunata being in a good temper that day, for she was going to a wedding party in the evening, and her thoughts were full of the glories of a certain spotted muslin that she had been most carefully iron-ing for the occasion. Signora Sunta was, as usual, sweet-tempered and unselfish. Alessio appeared grave and silent; Colomba, flushed and excited. She could not understand her lover's allowing their quarrel to last so long. And, by timid coquetries, she strove to open the way for him to make it up again. But he never even noticed her gentle blandish-ments, and thus filled her mind with wonder and dismay. By the time dinner was over she had grown quite uneasy; therefore, she hailed as a good omen Alessio's proposal that she should go with him into his studio.

She sat down opposite to him, but he did not long remain quiet, for he started to his feet and went to the window, apparently to scan the horizon. He could not bear to look at Colomba whilst he shamed her; and, heartless little flirt though he thought her, he knew that he should pain—at least her vanity. Till now he had thought that telling her would be a comparatively easy task, but now many doubts assailed him. He felt curious to see how this girl would bear his tidings; he had already seen how another bore them, but *she* was an angel, and more than a mere woman, he thought.

" Art thou still angry with me, oh, Alessio? How true is the proverb that says, ' Love and Jealousy were born together.' "

What effrontery in her to talk thus, as though they were still affianced! Her words so angered him that he found courage to commence his task. He turned half round, and said, gravely :—" Love and Jealousy may have been born together—and, if so, they certainly *die* together. As I feel no love for thee, Colomba, neither can I be angry or jealous."

"Alessio! tell me, art thou serious? I did not believe what thou saidst yesterday."

"And yet thou didst act as though thou believedst it well."

"What dost thou say?"

"I say that thou didst act as though thou wert a free girl!"

Colomba turned pale. What could he mean? "But thou art jealous?" she said, half plaintively.

"I tell thee, Colomba, I am not jealous. Arch-priest! will nothing make thee believe me, when I tell thee that I love thee not,—that thou art not for me!"

Colomba covered her face with her hands, and sobbed aloud.

To Alessio these appeared as crocodile's tears, and he became still more angry. He did not perceive that she was really troubled by the thought of the material comforts she would lose, and the fear of her parents' anger, and the shame and discomfort that awaited her. She felt humbled to the dust; she was indeed being punished for her sins. So she continued to cry miserably.

" Oh, woman, woman ! Truly do they say
—' who says woman, says evil '—and, ' those
who wish thee ill stroke thy skin ! ' *I* am no
longer deceived ; thou art not a dove, thou
art rather a serpent ! Why dost thou pretend to care for me when thou hast so fine
a gentleman for a lover ? "

Colomba started to her feet—" What ! "

" I say, thou hast a gentleman for a lover,
and I saw thee with him this morning. Take
good heed, Colomba, that he does not play
with thee ! He is affianced to a rich and
beautiful lady, and he does but divert himself with thee."

" Thou liest ! "

" I lie not ! I do but tell thee the truth. I
know where he lives, and where his betrothed
lives. I have spoken with her, and *I* sold
her the ring he gave thee so unwillingly."

" Thou insultest me ! Oh, holy Madonna,
hear thy child ! Is all the world combined to
mock and deceive me ? " and she sank back
into her chair, pale and quivering.

Alessio pitied her now, and he began to
repent his roughness. Usually gentle, it was
the thought of Ina that had made him so stern
to Colomba—and for this he was already

sorry. He approached her penitently; but she started to her feet with flashing eyes.

"Touch me not! Ah, thou liar! Thou cruel brigand, thou first insultest me thyself, and then pretendest that all other men are like to thee! But thou art wrong! My Carlo loves me! Yes! he loves me. And thy stories are worth nothing. He would not dare deceive me! And if he did—by all the saints in Heaven! I would kill him. Know, that it was my promise to thee that has kept me from encouraging him; but now I will become a grand lady—and what will a stupid ox of a goldsmith matter to me then!"

This abusive speech made her seem quite repulsive to Alessio, and he said to himself : — "Mercenary little wretch!" and again contrasted her with Ina. Still he could not let Colomba remain in this very dangerous frame of mind, for she appeared capable of committing any rash act. He must try and convince her of the truth. Her vanity blinded her, as much as Ina's innocence had blinded *her*, to the true character of Conte Carlo.

"I tell thee, Colomba, that the Conte would never marry thee; he is affianced."

" I tell thee, Alessio, that thou art a liar,
and I believe thee not ! "

" Will nothing convince thee ? "

" I must see it with my own eyes. Art
ready to take me to the house where his
affianced lives ? "

" I will conduct thee there ; but we cannot intrude upon the lady."

" Wilt take me ? "

What Colomba expected to gain by seeing
Ina's house is doubtful. Perhaps she did
not believe Alessio, and wished to try him ;
perhaps she believed more than she showed,
and wished for further evidence.

They walked in silence to the old painter's
house. Standing in front of it, Colomba
looked at the building suspiciously.

" Wilt thou go home now ? "

" No ! I will enter that carpenter's shop
in the old wall opposite, there to watch,"
said Colomba, resolutely. " If what thou
hast said is truth, he will come ; and if thou
art a liar, I shall see thee blush."

Suddenly, Alessio felt her grasp his arm,
and, following the direction of her eyes, he
saw the Conte leaving the house opposite ;
with a most dejected aspect. Colomba turned

pale as death, and her breath came in quick gasps.

She held Alessio until the Conte was out of sight, and then, dropping his arm, said in a hurried whisper : " And now we will go in and see *her*."

" Art mad ? "

" No! but I now think thou art not a liar, and I would know the whole truth. I hate thee—but not as I hate *him*, if he has deceived me. Thou wouldst have married me if I had treated thee better; thou hast never preferred another to me. But if he meant to play with me, and loved another, by Heaven—I will——"

" But were *you* not playing with him and with poor Bertoldo ? "

" That is another thing. Be silent, for I will not be further insulted ! "

Colomba crossed the street and gave a loud pull at Miss Laurence's bell. Alessio felt miserably embarrassed, and wished he had never brought her there. But if the servant admitted this little virago, the least he could do was to go in himself with her. Alas! the servant showed them in, and straight up into that very drawing-room where he had already been that morning. Ina sat there alone.

The change in her appearance gave Alessio quite a shock; for she already looked ten years older, so sad, so hopeless, was the expression of her beautiful face. She felt that she had received a mortal wound—and that all things were now indifferent to her. In her noble unselfishness, she had been willing to resign her lover, heart-breaking though it would be to lose him. But to resign her ideal, to find that her lover had never been truly hers, that she had given her heart to the most worthless of men—ah! *that* was indeed terrible agony. Now she felt a dull and hopeless despair.

At first, Conte Carlo had tried to laugh off her accusations and suggestions, treating them as jealous fancies; but at last, being angered by her persistency, he told her plainly that he was merely flirting with the girl, and that it was not her business to inquire into his conduct when away from her. She must not suppose that he never meant to look at another woman.

Then Ina, in her turn, grew indignant, and said that he could not deceive her; he must be in love with this other girl, and that he ought to marry her. At this he laughed, and said he would go to the Devil sooner! If Ina would not marry him herself, she had no right to dispose of him elsewhere; and he added some coarse and bad expressions that quite awoke her from all delusions regarding his character. She then told him proudly, that all was over between them. On her saying this, he retorted that he could easily find consolation elsewhere; the little contadina should amuse him.

But, as soon as he had left the room, the Conte regretted that his evil passions had got the better of his judgment, and thus, possibly, lost him so rich a prize. Why had he answered her so idiotically? So he left the house with a crestfallen mien, inwardly cursing his bad temper. But before he reached his own home, he had determined to pay her out. After all, it could only be a fit of jealousy.

Ina stood pale, calm, and silent like a statue — and seemingly as indifferent as marble itself. She did not even notice the two persons before her.

Colomba was astonished and awestruck—

she could not help admiring her rival, and, therefore, feared and disliked her the more.

Alessio was the first to break the silence. His melodious voice vibrated with intense sympathy, as he spoke :

" Oh, illustrious Signorina, forgive our intrusion, I pray you ! This young girl is the one of whom we spoke. She would not believe my words, therefore she has come to you—to hear that you are the betrothed of Conte Carlo."

When he spoke, Ina gave a start like one awakened from sleep. And on hearing his last words a slight shiver passed over her. She seemed to make a strong effort to collect her faculties, and then, looking wearily at Colomba, said in a strange, husky voice :

" I *was* the betrothed of Signor Conte Bentivoglio, but I am so no longer. I tried to induce him to marry you ; but he has no honour, and I could do nothing. I pity you —but what power have I ?—he was born to break our hearts."

"He has not broken mine ! Ah, the brigand ! so he would deceive me, play with me ! You may be a saint, Signorina, but I am a woman. Am I to remain on the little chair because of him, and be unmarried all my days? Are all men to deceive and slight me? Am I neither to have the position of a jeweller's wife, nor become a Contessa? Ohimè! I am most unfortunate!" And she flung herself into a chair, and sobbed violently.

Alessio had been looking from the flushed passionate face, to the pale and calm one, and thinking what a good picture they would make—they were such a complete contrast.

Ina made a gesture of repugnance towards Colomba, and murmured: "They are all alike. The world is full of the wicked, false, and mercenary—and I used to think it so good!"

"No! Signorina, the world is not all bad —it is mixed."

"But what can you say for him—for *her?*"

"For him, nothing! For her, that she is innocent, foolish, and ignorant; but not all bad."

"I do not understand it! *I* think she *is* all bad; for she deceived you, and all along only thought of self-interest, and never loved any one. It is, perhaps, better for one-self to have no heart, but——"

"No! Signorina, excuse me, but it is not better to have no heart. The more we suffer, the more noble we become. Love ever works for good. The base cannot understand unselfish grief, and it is so much the worse for them."

"What you say may be true; but, nevertheless, it is hard to suffer," and her lips quivered. She had forgotten Alessio's station as she talked with him. It was a moment of supreme emotion, and they spoke their thoughts freely, untrammelled by worldly distinctions.

"We must forgive this child, because she does not understand what is right. She is only seventeen, and quite uneducated."

"I cannot forgive a mercenary spirit."

But, even as she spoke, Ina's heart softened towards Colomba. The poor little thing's convulsive sobs had grown hysterical, and her figure shook with wild mirth and passionate grief. Ina took her in her arms, softly caressing her. And, strange to say, this had the effect of stopping her hysterics, so great was her surprise and pleasure. As she lay pale and trembling in her arms, Ina thought how pretty and young she looked.

She must be silly, she could not be bad.
The tender, gentle heart, so little prone to
imagine evil, relented. She regretted her hard
words, and kissed Colomba as affectionately
as she might have kissed a younger sister.

Alessio thought he had never seen anything
so angelic as the expression of Ina's face.
And he turned away quickly, unable to look
at her longer.

Colomba was also affected, touched,
amazed.

" Oh, Signorina ! " she said, in a weak
voice, " You are an angel, a saint! Let me
kiss your hand. Ah! may the Madonna
bless you ! "

"And may she bless you, too, poor little
one."

" Oh, no ! I am wicked, I have a devil in
my heart. I feel that I hate all men, and the
Conte most of all. I hold him in detestation
for his conduct to *you* as well as to me. *I*
would never have played with him had I
known he was yours; but *he knew*, and
therefore he was an ugly toad ! "

" It is no use abusing other people for
their faults, little one; we should rather try
to correct our own. You must never flirt

any more, but do your duty faithfully, and then, some day, you may marry a good man."

"I cannot think together of goodness and of men, for they are quite opposite! Oh! Signorina, forgive me! I am wicked; but I love you." And, impulsively kissing Ina's hand, Colomba rose to go. But she found herself so weak that she would have fallen had not Alessio assisted her.

"Good-bye," said Ina, gently and sadly.

Alessio looked at her with reverent admiration. "Good-bye, Signorina! Colomba is right; you are a true angel!"

"Alas, no!"

They went out after this.

Ina, going to her own room, lay down upon the sofa, with a weight as of lead on her heart. She said to herself: "I have lived my life—and what remains?—only Duty."

When they were out in the street, Colomba said hurriedly: "Take me home, Alessio, back to Fiesole. I will have no more of Florence!"

And so he took her home to her mother.

La Caterina looked at her daughter in fear and surprise. There was no luggage. Had she only come for an hour's visit!

"Colomba is not very well, Signora Caterina, let her go to bed now, and do me the pleasure not to question her."

Colomba kissed her mother, and went silently to her room.

"What is it, my Alessio?"

"Oh, Signora Caterina, my heart is heavy at having to tell thee; but I must proceed. Thy Colomba is foolish and young, and she loved me not, therefore she has been flirting with a Signore. All is over between us two; and I have brought her back for thee to take care of her. Ohimè! it was an ugly day when she came into the town!"

"Holy Virgin! most ugly! Oh, my child! my unfortunate one! Thou breakest my heart by thy news, Alessio! And was it her perfidy that made thee give her up?"

"No! she was not suited to me, and loved me not."

"I had feared that myself, Alessio mio."

"And then I found out that she was courting with a Conte. But, though he is a brigand, *she* is innocent."

"I thank Heaven!"

"And thou wilt comfort her?"

"Ah, yes! Poor little bird, who can love

her like her mother ? But my Simone will be enraged. Ah! this world, this world!"

"I will do anything in my power to content him."

"No! thou shalt not. Shalt thou pay us because we have spoilt our daughter, and her head is so full of nonsense that she cannot love an honest man ? Ah, no! it is thou who hast suffered most. *I* will bear all the reproaches."

"Thou art a good woman, Signora Caterina."

"I am a mother. Ah! my Alessio, thou knowest not what a mother feels——when the cruel hawk pursues the tender little birds, do not their parents defend them, even to the death—dying whilst covering their children with their wings ? Even so would I do. To have my little one back safe is great joy! No hawk can touch her here—she is in my arms, on my heart, and love makes me strong. Ah, blessed, blessed little Colomba, flower of my soul! Woe to those who would wrong thee, or think evil of thee! When thou art safe with me——ah! I can bear anything."

"She ought never to have left thee, Signora. We took not sufficient care of her.

We meant all for the best, but we gave her too much liberty."

"Thou didst not understand her, Alessio. I have been suffering from many fears, but *now* I am content. Go home, my son, go home! *I* will care for her now. Rest tranquil; all is for the best."

"Happiest night, mother! I go to see Bertoldo."

"Ah! poor man, he too has suffered."

"*He* loves Colomba yet, and I think she likes *him* best. Who knows? all may yet make a good end." And with that comforting idea, Alessio left her.

Poor Caterina! She had to soothe an angry husband and try to comfort her child. Colomba was at present sullen and cross, and she utterly refused to open her heart to her mother, and would tell her nothing. Certainly, Caterina's lot was far from enviable. But she prayed many prayers to the Madonna asking her to help her, and she felt much comforted before she closed her eyes in sleep.

Colomba did not rest quietly; for in her heart was the desire to revenge herself, and she planned how best to accomplish this end.

CHAPTER IV.

VENGEANCE.

AT last Colomba was thoroughly convinced of Conte Carlo's perfidy. It had been difficult to make her believe him false; for the idea was most unflattering to her vanity. The Italians are not, as a rule, a vain people, for pride takes the place of vanity in them. Colomba, contadina though she was, possessed her share of pride; but she had also a perfect faith in the power of her personal attractions. She had been flattered by the attentions of a gran Signore; but she had never doubted that he would be glad to marry her, if she would have him. She had not meant to do so, however, as she was then betrothed to Alessio. She was far too innocent and good to suspect him of any bad intentions towards her—and she was too proud to think that he merely wished to flirt with her. Now that she understood that he had been amusing himself with her, and that he had all along been affianced to another, her pride was aroused, and bitter was her anger and mortification. She had asked Alessio to take her home; and now that she was there, she found time to realize to the full the misery of her position.

She was crouching alone near the window, with pale cheeks and wild eyes, staring aimlessly at the summer landscape. She had refused to listen to a word of comfort from her mother, and had only begged to be left alone. Poor Caterina had wept many tears that evening, before she went to bed, and had prayed so devoutly to the Virgin—she feared that her poor child's heart was broken, and that it was the Conte she had loved, not Bertoldo. In reality, it was Colomba's pride and ambition that were wounded, not her heart and affections. As yet the wilful child seemed to have no love to spare for any one but herself. She was still unconscious of the slight preference she had always cherished for poor Bertoldo—the lover she had treated with the greatest contempt.

In fact, she was unable to understand the suffering she had caused Bertoldo and Alessio; for she had not loved the Conte, and, therefore, did not know that wounded love gives even worse pain than wounded vanity. She fancied that what they had suffered was as nothing compared to her own misery. The bitter thought of having been deceived, of having lost two good matches, was as wormwood to her. She did not see in the Conte's behaviour a just retribution for her own conduct towards her two other lovers.

"Oh! Dio mio! how unfortunate am I! To be treated like the dust of the earth, to be played with as a girl of no account! Was it for this that I dismissed poor Bertoldo, and made small account of that good Alessio! For this—to be cast aside by a brigand who never loved me! Am I to remain with no husband at all in the end! Holy Virgin! it renders me mad, thus to have been made a fool of. But—" and her eyes blazed forth dark lightnings, and she clenched her tiny fist—"But, shall I then permit it! Shall he laugh at me as well as at the poor Signorina Inglese, who is an angel? Shall he tell his

friends of the little contadina who caused
him such excellent diversion ? Ah, no!
mille diavoli! this shall never be. Am I to
bear with patience that the neighbours
should laugh about me as the girl who
flirted, and whom no one will ever marry ?
No, no ! Colomba Vestris was never made
to eat her own heart in silence. She will be
revenged, and the false traitor shall pay her
account with the blood of his ugly heart ! "

There was an intent look in her eyes now;
for she was planning how she could best
accomplish her vengeance. Colomba knew
that her father and mother were too gentle
and timid to help her; she was too proud to
ask Bertoldo's aid ; and she felt that Alessio
was too good to have anything to do with a
blood-thirsty design. Yes! with her own
hands, she must accomplish her revenge.
When the Conte was dead, they should not
send her to the galleys—life was ended for
her, since she had been thus slighted, and
disappointed in all her ambitious hopes.
She would first assassinate the perfidious
one, and then kill herself. How to do
the deed was her present difficulty. And
she sat there, pondering, until the sun had

sunk in angry splendour, and a dark, starless night had enveloped all things. Then she shivered, and, closing the window, crept silently into bed.

Colomba slept but lightly that night; bad dreams troubled her, and she tossed from side to side. Her last dream was of hurling something down upon some one, and she awoke with the death-cry ringing in her ears.

This dream was an out-birth of her own excited thoughts; and yet, strange to say, it was this very dream that showed her how she could best accomplish her revenge.

Her room was close to the small terrace where she kept her flower-pots; and, as her door opened upon the entry near the terrace, she considered it as her own sitting-room. It was this same terrace to which Bertoldo had mounted when he gave her the kiss. Colomba had one privilege connected with it; namely, that it gave her the power to leave the house whenever she chose without her parents having any knowledge of the fact—but she was not naughty enough to use this power—though she liked to feel that she possessed it.

The first thing she did on this morning, was to rise from her bed and hunt for a sheet of white paper, a quill pen, and a bottle of ink. With compressed lips and frowning brows, she sat down and wrote a letter. The characters were very straggling and shaky, and the spelling far from faultless; but the import of the letter was plain enough. The little traitress told the Conte that she could no longer meet him near the iron bridge or in the Cascine; but, if he loved her, he could come to see her at her own house. She gave the exact direction, and told him to come at eight o'clock in the evening, and to go round by the back-way and stand beneath the terrace, where she would meet him.

She folded up and wafered the letter, writing "Conte Carlo" on the outside. And then she began to puzzle her brains to think of some one to deliver it for her. She feared that she might be watched; but she forgot that Alessio had heard the rendezvous appointed between her and the Conte, and that he might, therefore, watch the Conte also.

All that day Colomba stayed in her room with the door locked, and old Simone stormed and swore outside, in vain. He longed to beat her, but was too miserly to break the lock open. Poor Caterina cried outside, also in vain; for Colomba's heart was hardened, and she was deaf to the voice of the softer emotions. In the evening she stole out to look for a messenger, and nearly encountered her angry father. So she ran back to her room in despair.

The next morning she again rose early, and had better luck, as she thought. She met a young lad, who, for the reward of a franc, gladly consented to wait for the Conte in the Cascine, give him her letter, and keep the whole matter secret.

She had not seen Alessio since he brought her home, for he had sent her box by one of his workmen. All the day long she lived in a fever of suspense, still keeping her room; but eating some of the food her mother left outside her door. Towards evening this suspense turned to a wild excitement, and at seven o'clock she already stood waiting on the terrace.

" It is certain that I am about to do a righteous deed; for I shall exterminate a devil ! "

As the moments sped on, her rage grew, and her determination became stronger. She longed to put an end to the wretch who had tried to deceive her; and she felt that it would be no more than he deserved. She exulted exceedingly in being the one who had lured him to his doom. And so she stood there—calm, resolute, and vigilant.

We English should consider such a girl a regular little fiend in human form, but we should be judging her as an English girl, and from our own standpoint of right and wrong. Colomba was of a far more passionate nature than ours, and of a people who have still much of the pagan element in them. She was only about to do what many of her countrywomen had done before her. And she took the matter in a business-like and cold-blooded way that would have made it appear to us all the more revolting.

At last Colomba heard a footstep on the stones below. The night was dark; but she leaned over, and could dimly distinguish the figure of a man standing exactly beneath the wall of the terrace. Her heart beat faster as she said softly—" Die traitor !" at the same time laying her hand on an enormous flower-pot just above the place where the man stood. She was pushing it slowly to the edge, when a hand caught hers—not in time to prevent the fall of the pot, but in time to break the force of its descent. The pot rebounded and broke against the wall before it reached the ground.

There was a sudden sharp cry, and the man was no longer standing below.

Colomba turned and saw Alessio, white and stern, standing beside her, holding her hand as in a vice.

" Unfortunate and wicked girl, what hast thou done? Thou hast assassinated him ! "

" I had that intention ! " she cried, exultantly.

" Oh, mad one ! It is not the Conte thou hast killed ! *I* took thy letter from the boy, and met the Conte myself—I spoke strongly to him, and made him promise not to seek thee. Ah ! accursed is the devil that has entered into thy heart and made thee assassinate an innocent man ! "

" I do not believe it ! " But her cheeks turned pale, and she trembled in every limb.

Alessio fetched the lamp from Colomba's

E 2

bedroom, and, keeping hold of her hand, forced her to descend the steps with him. All the stern resolve and passion, that had made her act like a little Jael, had now entirely left her—and she was but a terrified, miserable girl, little more than a child in years and intelligence.

They approached the prostrate man, and Alessio bent down and held the lamp to his face—and then they saw—Bertoldo !

With a low wail of pain, Colomba flung herself down beside him, and kissed his still face in so wildly passionate a manner that Alessio feared she had gone mad.

" Oh ! I have killed him ! I have killed thee, thee, my poor Bertoldo ! This hand that thou lovedst has caused thy death. Oh ! accursed that I am ! Heaven wills that I should be punished for my sins, and sends me the agony of being the assassin of my Bertoldo. Truly, the hand that tried to stop me was indeed an angel's—but *Fate* was against me—it was my destiny, and nothing could prevent this misery. Oh ! beloved, beloved ! I know, now that I have killed thee, that thou hast ever been my heart's love. Ohimè ! ohimè ! misera mè ! Holy

Virgin, take my soul into Purgatory, for I am no longer worthy to live, now that I have killed my Bertoldo."

"Let me come to him, Colomba; I do not think he is really dead."

Alessio sprinkled water on the insensible Bertoldo's face. And, lo! he opened his eyes, and saw Colomba bending over him.

"Ah! Diavoletta, wert thou not content with breaking my heart, that thou must needs break my head also?"

"Oh! Bertoldo, I did not know it was thee."

"I am not entirely certain of that. Any way, I can make a processo* against thee."

"As thou wilt. Have me punished; send me to the galleys for life; it matters not to me; for my heart is full of joy now that *thou* art not dead! Oh, Alessio! it was indeed an angel in thy form that saved me from a life of remorse."

"Would it have mattered to *thee* if I had died?" asked Bertoldo, sitting up, and looking at her eagerly.

"It would have mattered much to me— the galleys would have been the least of my

* Law-suit.

misfortunes—the greatest, to lose thee."
And she arose with a blush, and turned to
go into the house.

But in an instant Bertoldo was beside
her, showing by his activity that he was not
much hurt; for, thanks to Alessio's interven-
tion, he had only received some bruises and
a cut on the head. He caught Colomba's
hands in his, and held her captive.

Alessio walked quietly away. Leaving
the yard, he returned to his own house in
Florence. He felt quite easy in his mind
now; for he knew there would be no further
tragedy.

" Tell me, Colombina of my heart, dost
thou love me ? "

" I love thee, Bertoldo."

He clasped her in a warm embrace, and
his heart was comforted at last.

" What wert thou doing down there,
Bertoldo ? "

" I desired to be near *thee ;* that was all."

" Ah ! thou dost not know how wicked
I have been," she said, timidly.

"Yes, I know all."

" And is it possible that thou still lovest
me ? "

"Thou hadst my heart, Colomba, and I could not, if I would, call it back again. I cannot help loving thee, most beautiful one! I know that thou hast not loved me as I have thee—but I have loved all the more, to make it equal."

Truly, poor Bertoldo had been much changed and improved by his love and sorrow. And Colomba felt ashamed of her own unworthiness as she listened to his words. She inwardly vowed that she would honour, love, and obey him all the days of her life.

Long did the lovers linger there, saying sweet nothings. Colomba had begged to be forgiven, and had been forgiven with many a loving word and caress. At last she said, playfully:

"Thou wilt not send me to prison?"

"The only prison I have for thee is here in my arms, upon my heart, beloved. For thou must marry me soon, Colomba."

"I will marry thee, Caro, when thou wilt."

"Ah! heart's desire, thou knowest my wish—it is to have thee as soon as possible. Let us now go to ask thy parents' consent."

Greatly did Simone and Caterina re-joice over this new engagement. They had been sitting together, dolefully picturing to themselves the condition of their unfor-tunate child, who, they imagined, was crying alone in her room. When, lo! the door opened, and two radiant young persons entered, and asked their blessing upon their betrothal.

Colomba threw her arms around her mother's neck, and, with tears of joy, told her that she was perfectly happy now; and that she was sorry for her past naughtiness, and hoped that her mother would forgive her.

Caterina knew that her daughter would be happy now; for she had chosen the husband best suited to her.

Old Simone muttered to himself: "She might have made a richer match if she had been prudent; but, as she is an idiot of a woman, it is best that she take him, else she might remain without any husband in the end."

Bertoldo went home that night with a heart full of the most perfect content and thankfulness. He did not see Colomba's faults—because he loved her blindly—but even his love, such as it was, was strong to save. For, as Colomba laid her head on the pillow that night she said to herself: "Holy Madonna, I thank thee! Thou hast blessed me beyond my deserts. Thou hast saved me from misery, and there is no longer the evil passion of revenge in my heart. To me, now, the Conte matters not. I can think of nothing but my Bertoldo. I will cook him the best of dinners, keep his house as clean as possible, and be to him a docile and obedient wife. Oh! Holy Saints, bless him; for he is good and faithful—the sweetest cake in all the world. I will love him all my life until I die, and my soul goes to thee, Holy Madonna."

CHAPTER V.

COLOMBA'S WEDDING.

IT was a bright summer's day when Alessio was awakened by a loud knocking at his bedroom door. On his saying " Passate " (Come in), a rough-headed peasant lad entered hastily.

" What do you want, friend?" asked Alessio, sleepily.

" Excuse me, Signor Pittore, is it not the truth that you have been invited to the wedding of la Colomba Vestris this day?"

" Certainly, friend; but why wake me before eight o'clock, when the Mass is fixed for the hour of eleven?"

" Yes, yes, Signore; it was fixed thus; but the good priest says he is hungry and weak, and cannot wait for so long; the ceremony must take place before ten."

Alessio laughed, as he gave the boy ten centimes, and sent him out of the room. But the priest's message did not seem by any means so strange to him, as it would to us.

Alessio was utterly without regret with respect to Colomba; and he indulged in no sentimental memories. The whole idea had been a dream—a creation of Fata Morgana —from which he had been awakened most completely. His only feeling was one of pleasure, at the thought of Bertoldo's happiness.

So, it was with a light heart that he dressed himself in his best clothes—in honour of the wedding.

"Where art thou going, Alessio mio?" asked his mother, tenderly.

"To the wedding of Colomba and Bertoldo."

"Listen to this story! Thus goes the world! Thou dressest thyself like a prince, nephew, to adorn the wedding of thy sweetheart! Truly, thou hast little respect for thyself."

"Silence, silence, dear aunt!" said Alessio, good-humouredly; "have I not told both you and my mother, that I myself broke

off my marriage with Colomba Vestris. This
being the case, I am glad to see her wed my
friend, the good Bertoldo."

"It is not true—not a word of it! Ah!
no, I know the world better than you think,
nephew. You cannot deceive me." And
Fortunata tossed her head incredulously as
she left the room. But, though her private
opinion was, that Colomba had treated
Alessio very badly, and that he had not shown
half enough spirit,—yet she expressed herself in public after a very different fashion—
saying to the sposa next door: "That was a
worthless girl, Colomba Vestris : our Alessio
was forced to give her up; but he has a good
heart, he would not let her die an old maid;
so he found her a partito in his friend,
Bertoldo. And he goes to their wedding
to show every one that he approves of the
match. Yes, our Alessio is a good boy!"

"Our Alessio" was now seated in a fly
driving to Fiesole as fast as possible—
having due regard for the good priest's
hunger.

The last time he had been on that road it
was for a very different purpose, and he
could hardly realize that so short a time ago

he had been speeding to Fiesole to save
Colomba from a great crime; whilst now he
was going to rejoice at her wedding.

Such is life—comedy and tragedy inter-
woven as woof and warp.

Alessio went to Bertoldo's house, and
proceeded with him to the church, where
they found the rest of the wedding party
awaiting them.

Bertoldo was nervous, but beaming with
happiness. Colomba looked rather pale,
but very beautiful. She was dressed in black
silk, and wore a lovely set of gold ornaments
that Alessio had given her as a wedding
present. Catera was tearful — the father
triumphant. All the guests were pleased,—
for they knew that the good Catera had provided an ample feast.

Colomba smiled gratefully when she saw
Alessio—though she inwardly wondered at
his pleased and tranquil air, and realized,
with a pang, that he did not regret her. But
this was only a momentary feeling of
wounded vanity, and she was really glad to
see him happy. She loved Bertoldo as well
as she could love, and was quite content.
The Conte was forgotten—she only thought

of her sposo now, and of her own promotion in becoming a wife.

The sun shone brightly upon the happy party, and the Mass was proceeding quietly; when suddenly, just in the middle, a great clamour was heard in the Piazza outside— the barking of a dog and the shouts of boys.

The hungry priest turned sharp round from the altar, and exclaimed: " Oh! who the Devil could do anything with such an accursed row? Be off, some of you, and clear me that Piazza; or, by Bacchus! I shall leave the altar. Via! I say." *

Away scampered a dozen ragged little boys at full speed down the church; and the uproar became worse than ever.

Bertoldo turned red, and Colomba bit her lip with vexation. But Alessio walked out quietly, and restored order in the Piazza— returning with the *guardia nobile* to witness the end of the interrupted ceremony.

When the Mass was concluded, Bertoldo went to pay the fees, leaving Colomba standing by her mother.

Then, a rush of all the gamins towards the door took place; and they nearly massacred

* A fact.

each other as a shower of confetti (sugar-plums) was rattled upon their heads by the bride's relations and friends.

Mortars were fired off at intervals all day —and, in fact, there was a general Festa. In the evening a band played, and there was a dance in the Piazza.

The dancers were mostly peasants, who had been invited by Catera and her husband to Colomba's wedding. The Piazza was illuminated by oil lamps—and a bright moon shone down on the merry-makers.

Some of the dances were pretty, but the quadrilles ended in universal chaos, and the waltzes had a churning movement far from graceful. A friendly sergeant of infantry, in military uniform, directed the dances in French technical phraseology, and danced like a possédé.

The supper arrangements were peculiar— as all the guests walked off to the Trattoria, where tables were laid, and paid for their own rations, entertaining the Vestris into the bargain.

The ancient matrons of the party were silent to a degree, and, being all strictly classified in a row, they looked just like so many criminals awaiting capital punishment.

The young women were very sober, and also
sat in long files, holding no social inter-
course with their partners.   The young men
clustered outside the door in passages, and
made no attempt at conversation.   The pre-
vailing air was of deep gravity and careworn
seriousness, though they were all really happy.
After supper, dancing began again, and a
very pretty country-dance was enacted.   It
represented a courtship in pantomime, most
expressively pressed and rejected.   The girl
always eluding her partner's outstretched
hands, and escaping gracefully from his
advances until he retired worn out, to be
replaced by another swain, who gained the
day by beseeching the lady's favour in a
wonderful figure danced *on his knees*.
Nothing could have been prettier than the
defiant snap-of-the-finger way in which the
little contadina flew away from the rejected
partner, or the gracious, relenting reception
she gave the humble admirer on his knees,
and the final clasping of hands over their
heads as they danced together the last steps.

Alessio stood silently watching the others'
enjoyment.   He looked rather pale and sad ;
seeming the one apart.   A hand touched his,

and, turning, he saw Colomba looking up at him with beaming eyes.

"Art thou happy, Colomba?"

"Oh! so happy, Alessio, that I fear to breathe the word, lest it should all vanish at a touch."

"May it continue a thousand years! I wish thee every good. But now, Colombina, you must excuse me, as I have to return to Florence."

Colomba hesitated, then, blushing crimson, she added hastily: "And *I* wish that you may one day invite me to your wedding; and that you may be as happy as we are—for, surely, you have deserved it much more than I."

Alessio sighed, but he thanked her gently, and, kissing her hand, stepped out into the darkness alone.

"That page is turned," he thought; "Colomba and Bertoldo have a new life before them. But for me — is my life finished? I must no longer place my faith in la Fata Morgana, and build palaces in the sky. But, oh! Dio mio! if *this* love is a dream, let me die still a dreamer. The English poet Shakespeare says: 'It were all one that I should love a bright particular star, and think to wed it.' And even so is she to me—as ' a bright particular star ' ; she shall guide me and light my path. My footsteps shall no longer stumble 'neath the glow of a meaner light. This may still be Fata Morgana; it can but be ideal—but it shall be eternal. Good-bye to you both, Colomba and Bertoldo ! Simple, happy souls, you could not even understand my feelings— in my world I am alone."

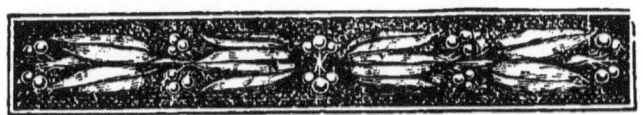

CHAPTER VI.

ALESSIO'S QUEEN.

INA'S life was now very desolate; she tried in vain to sing or paint, and at last gave up the struggle as fruitless. From a sad habit, she often walked to her window to look out, and then, recollection returning to her, would sigh and turn away.

She felt her loss far more deeply than Alessio had felt his; for his awakening had been gradual—hers a more sudden blow. And then, woman-like, she had staked her all on the cast of a die. She had seen her beautiful dream fade as a mirage in the desert—and now only the desert seemed left to her.

Alessio had his Art to comfort him. And then, he had also the germ of a true and noble love in his heart—a love that could but die with that heart itself. His fancy for

Colomba had been but a vain imagination;
Ina's for Carlo was a mistaken and romantic
idealization of an unworthy object, but still
there had been more personal preference
in it.

Ina was a noble woman, and she did not
mean to spend her life in useless regret; but
she felt she needed a change, so she determined to leave Florence, where everything
around her reminded her of her sorrow.

Mrs. Hume was delighted with Ina's
desire for change, and gladly helped her in
her preparations for departure. For, though
sincerely sorry for her niece, she was still
more sorry for herself; and, as she told
Signor Minuti: "A girl suffering from
blighted affections is not the liveliest companion in the world!" In addition to her
home troubles, Mrs. Hume was at present
suffering from outside worries. A great
celebrity had visited Florence, and, on Mrs.
Hume's hastening to pay her respects to the
lion, she had received a most decided snub-
bing. And, moreover, many Italian grandees,
who had formerly courted her for her niece's
sake, now quietly dropped her; for they
knew that Ina had " turned melancholy," and

that she refused to go into society. Therefore Mrs. Hume agreed eagerly with her
niece's proposal; and they began at once to
prepare for their departure.

Alessio was quite cheerful now; for he felt
that he had escaped from a great danger.
He had never been calmly happy during his
engagement; it had been but a troubled
pleasure—a rose with many thorns.

He set himself to work with new energy
and earnestness—he must do his part in life,
and no longer dally with Art.

Both Colomba and her husband regarded
Alessio as their best friend, and considered
that they owed their happiness to him.
Fortunata still expressed great indignation
when speaking of Colomba, and, though she
had spoken loudly against the match, she now
spoke just as loudly against "the flirt" who
had slighted her nephew; though she added,
"She was glad Alessio had shown sufficient
sense to get rid of the little fool!"

Alessio visited Signor Minuti's studio
constantly, and always managed to ask
after the Signorina Laurence. Soon the old
painter learnt to save time and trouble by
proffering the desired information. Alessio

was grieved to hear of the continued sadness and despondency of the young lady, and of her altered appearance.

One day Signor Minuti called at Alessio's house to speak to him. He was ushered into the parlour by la Fortunata, who told him that her nephew was out, and asked him if he would sit down and wait.

" Certainly, Signorina, if I do not incommode you : "—said the old man, with an amused twinkle in his eyes, for he knew that she dearly loved a gossip with him. And he, for his part, was not averse to this unintellectual occupation. For he was sufficiently English in taste to derive amusement from the quaintness and originality of his country-people—that is, of the lower classes.

" Ah! I am already half dead ! I have ironed all this blessed day ! But, it is my destiny. However, I can sit with you to divert you for a moment, Signore, though, as you know, I have always much to do, and my health is most miserable. Patience ! "

" Certainly ; you are a most amiable woman to bear your misfortunes with such a holy patience," he replied, in a tone of grave sympathy, but really with secret mirth.

La Fortunata was gratified, so she said amiably—" Ah! Signor Pittore, you are troppo garbato! You are not like the other men, who do not understand us women. You are such good company, you always cause me to laugh, and—'every time one laughs, one takes a nail from one's coffin!' Would you credit it, Signore, this morning in the omnibus I beheld a marvel, and had occasion to remark what an extraordinary nation are the English! They are not civilized at all, and we may truly call them barbarians."

" You render me curious, in truth! Tell me, Signorina, what did you see?"

" I will tell you the whole story. At the Piazza della Signoria, I stepped into the omnibus with the intention of going to the Santa Croce. All the places were occupied, except one, and we were just going on—when lo! some one called to the driver, and entered the omnibus. It was an English lady. I must say, she was a fine piece of woman-kind, fat, and with a beautiful colour on her face. Her hair was grey, and all curled, and she was dressed well enough, in some purple cashmere stuff. To look at her, you would

have said—'That is a lady'; but you will
hardly believe me when I tell you that this
lady carried in her hand *a large basket.*
Fancy the shame! I blushed for her. Why
could she not have carried a red spotted
handkerchief of cotton, such as I do? It
would have been much more decent. As
you well know, Signore, no respectable
Italian woman would ever consent to carry
a basket. But this shameless one sat down
as though it was nothing, with that ugly
basket on her lap. I looked around the
omnibus, and all the other women gave me
glances, and we stared at the Inglese—who
never noticed us. At last we grew ashamed
for her, as she sat near the door, and the
persons in the street could see her. So we
began to make her signs to put her basket
under the seat;—she did not seem to understand us at all, and stared at us as though we
were all so many mad ones. We continued
to make signs, and the stupid Inglese to stare.
At last, she turned to me, and said:

"'What do you all want?'

"'It is the basket, Signora,' said I.

"'What do you want with my basket?'
returns she.

" 'Want it! Mammà mia! Oh, no, Signora! We meant that you might like to put it under the seat ? '

" 'Why should I put it under the seat ? '

" 'Because a Signora should not be seen carrying a basket, and we are all ashamed for you.'

" On that, the idiot burst out laughing, and held her basket tighter than ever. And we all thought within ourselves :—'How indecent are the English!' "

The painter concealed his amusement at this characteristic anecdote, and said gravely : —" But, Signorina, in different Lands there are different customs. In England the ladies all carry baskets, and only common labourers carry spotted handkerchiefs ;—the ladies there would be ashamed to carry a bundle."

La Fortunata shook her head, and muttered—" They are barbarians."

" We have had a good harvest this year," said Signor Minuti, by way of changing the subject.

" Pretty well, Signore; but the people of the country round Pistoja have had a bad sowing of the seed ; the rain began too early.

They prayed to the image of their patron saint to stop the accursed rain; but he would not listen to them. Then they told him they would beat him if he did not attend to them; but he was still obstinate;—so they beat him — but he was like an ox, most obstinate. So they put him down a well, to see if that would make him hear reason."

" And did he? "

" In effect, he did. And after ten days the rain ceased."

" And what became of the poor saint? "

" Oh! they took him out of the well, dried him, and put him back in the church. As he was of wax, some of his colour was spoilt, but it will be a good lesson for him, and teach him not to be so obstinate another time."

" We must hope that he will profit by experience," said the painter gravely. "And, did I not hear that the picture of the Madonna of the Church of the Santissima Anunziata is wonderful in its power of stopping the rain, when it is exhibited? "

" Yes, truly; but it needs a very bad harvest for the people to have courage to bring that forth, as it costs them so much. They have to pay three hundred lire, or perhaps even seven, — I am not exactly certain, but I know it is a large sum,—to the Municipio, for permission to have the picture uncovered."

"Then the Government actually taxes the Virgin?"

"Yes, the brigands! They say that if we receive a grace we must pay for it; and we do that thoroughly. First comes the bad season, then the Municipio with their tax, and then all who go to pray to the Madonna offer her a piece of money as alms to her church. Thus, it appears to me, that we pay well for a little grace. I cannot help telling of this, for, as you know, 'the tongue strikes where the tooth hurts.'"

At that moment Alessio entered, and greeted his friend warmly.

"I wish thee to come to walk with me. Canst thou, my son?"

"With pleasure, Signore."

"Good-bye, to meet again, Signorina."

And the two men stepped out into the street together.

"I wish to walk on the Viale dei Colli," said Signor Minuti, putting his arm through Alessio's.

It was now the beginning of winter, and the day was cold and clear. The sun shone brightly, and everything seemed to sparkle with a glad and vigorous life. They walked to the Colli by the Porta Romana, and, as they lingered on " the most beautiful drive in Europe" (as the Florentines call it), they admired the broad, expansive view before them. It was less extensive than the view from Fiesole, but even more picturesque.

"Oh! my son, thou canst not tell how thankful I am that thou hast escaped that little contadina. Think of the many great men who have suffered from unequal marriages!"

"I am not a great man."

"Not yet, but thou wilt become one. Thou hast it in thee. Thou wilt be considered a good painter whilst thou art in life, and a great one when thou art dead. And to think that a little contadina might have turned a genius into a simple shopman! I am glad, however, that her wayward little bark has reached the shore in safety. She was a pretty child, I grant—but she was not for thee;— 'too dear is that honey that one licks from thorns'!"

" Yes, she is safe now, and quite happy. She and Bertoldo suit each other to a marvel ; and she is improving every day. Bertoldo says that she tries hard to learn to be a good house-wife, but, as yet, she makes mistakes—for she is very ignorant. But she has good-will, and he is content. 'To every bird its own nest is beautiful.' "

" *Requiescat in pace.* Being, as the English say, ' off with your old love,' do not begin looking out for a new ! It is not likely you will ever find a woman to suit you, and I may truly say of artists—' Who marries does *well*, and who marries *not* does *better.*' "

" But, Signore, *you* married ! "

" I am not a *great* painter. But, to tell the truth, I would rather have had my poor Mary than have been a Michael Angelo."

" And may I not feel the same ? "

" First, you must find an angel like Mary ; and there are not many of that kind in the world."

" Ah, yes ! Signore, I shall never marry. I will only love my Art—Art shall be my wife."

The old painter smiled rather sadly.

They had by this time reached the Piazza
Michael Angelo on the Colli, with its statue
of David adorning the centre. They paused
near the marble balustrade, looking at the
prospect before them. Suddenly the painter
felt Alessio give a start of surprise, and
following the direction of his eyes, he saw a
young lady dressed in black sitting on a
marble bench near. She was gazing dreamily
at the distant city; he recognized Ina
Laurence.

Alessio had not seen her since their
memorable interviews, and he noted the
change in her appearance with sympathetic
pity. Signor Minuti approached her, still
holding Alessio's arm.

" Good-day, Signor Minuti. How you
startled me—I did not see you coming ! "

She took no notice of Alessio, who sat down
on the further end of the bench, as Signor
Minuti placed himself between them.

" Why are you contemplating Florence so
earnestly ? "

" Because I am wishing it good-bye. I
may never see it again, and I would carry
away its picture in my heart."

Alessio started ; he felt a sudden spasm

of pain. He had not heard of the projected departure before, and he could not bear the idea—*why*, he could not have said.

"You leave soon?"

"In three days."

"Are you glad to go?"

"Yes, and no! But I dearly love fair Florence; it is a city that seems to find the way to one's heart. See those distant blue hills, and the Duomo and Campanile shining in the sunlight, all so wide, clear, and grand. Why is the world so beautiful and yet so sad? Why are we so bad and life so good? It seems to me inharmonious, and it saddens my spirit."

"What is your opinion, Alessio?" said the painter, wishing to bring the young man into the conversation—and willing that Ina should hear some of his thoughts. It was well that Alessio did not notice the gesture of impatience that Ina gave, when Signor Minuti appealed to him. The reason for this movement on her part was, that the young man recalled painful memories, and so his very presence was disagreeable to her.

He answered gravely and simply; his rich

voice falling and rising in a melodious cadence, almost as though he were reciting.

"It seems to me, Signore, that the world is not all good, or all bad, any more than are its inhabitants. It is but the outward symbol of our natures, and everything in life has some counterpart in us. See that blue sky, without cloud or reflection—such is Life. But the clouds will come, tender pink first, for joy—that is Love; then the dark shade, for Sorrow; then the long night, for Death and parting—then will the sun arise with new splendour, as our souls will float in Paradise, free, enraptured, and blessed. Ah, Signore, I love the world; I love Nature in all her aspects, grand, wide, and bountiful. God gives it to us to take us out of ourselves, to console us, to bring our thoughts to Him; and to teach us to be thankful."

"Thou art right, my son. What think you, Ina; is he not a poet?"

"I think he is more religious than I am," said Ina, with half-grudging praise. She did not even like to hear the sound of his voice; and his words seemed like a rebuke to her. But she could not help owning that there was truth in what he said.

" Oh, no ! Signorina. I am sure you are far more religious than I. I have so many faults, and I fear that I have not considered these subjects enough. But I love the good God and all His works, as you do also, no doubt."

" If bad men are God's works, I do *not* love all His works ! " replied Ina, sharply.

" Little babies are God's works, and they are innocent. We have free will, I believe, and it is the wickedness of our own hearts that makes us bad. The created world is so beautiful, on purpose to make us good and contented; only we will not see it aright."

" I do not understand such things ; and I feel too unhappy to consider them," said she, with a sigh.

Just then an empty carriage drove up, and Ina said to the old painter : " Will you not come back with me to dinner ? "

"I do not like to leave my friend," replied he, hesitating, and secretly wishing Ina and Mrs. Hume were not too proud to invite Alessio.

" Have no care for me; I shall do quite well, Signore. You lose the Signorina so soon, every hour of her company must be precious. Good-day ! "

And, taking off his hat to them, with a bright smile, he walked away. Ina bowed coldly, and went with Signor Minuti to the carriage. Then—turning suddenly, she followed Alessio.

"Forgive me!" she said, gently, "if I have seemed unkind or rude to you. I am so unhappy! You were right in all you said, and, please God, I shall yet grow to think as you do." And she held out her hand to him. He touched it reverently --timidly. She then left him, and seated herself in the carriage by the side of the astonished Signor Minuti.

When they had driven out of sight, Alessio still remained standing where Ina had parted from him. There was a strange radiance in the expression of his face, as he murmured to himself: "For that lady I could die! She *touched* this hand. I swear that it shall achieve great things in honour of her! And I pray to God that it may never be sullied by an evil deed, or become unworthy of the hand that has touched it. She is a queen among women, and *I* am her servant *for ever.*"

"Well, Ina, I am glad that you have met

him. I wished you to know more of him. *He* is the genius I told you of. Do you not think him a fine fellow?"

"There is one thing puzzles me, Signor Minuti; he looks like a man who could really love, and—*he* was engaged to the little peasant who has married some one else; and yet—he does not seem to mind it. Is that the effect of his religion, or what?"

"He is a good and pious young man, I grant. But I must admit that I do not think he had much to bear in this case. We painters are an imaginative race, and too often make ourselves miserable for life by our fancies. He has had an escape, and knows it."

"I cannot understand that; I think people love—or do not love. There must be a want of depth in his character."

"That there is not! It is its very depth that makes Alessio's nature capable of a grand and noble love, and also gives him the power to cast aside a rootless fancy, created by his poetic imagination."

"It may be as you say; but I do not understand him. And though he seems an interesting character, I own I never wish to see him again ; for the sight of him is painful to me."

" Poor fellow ! "

" It is not his fault. After all, it can matter to no one ; for we are in such different spheres of life that we shall never again meet each other."

" I think you are in different spheres ! " said the painter, indignantly. " *He* is in the paradise of Art, and is filled by noble aspirations—whilst *you*, poor child, are stumbling in the Slough of Despond." Signor Minuti would hardly have spoken so strongly to Ina if he had heard her last words to Alessio ; but, as it was, he was growing impatient with what seemed to him her intolerable pride.

" Anyway, I shall be in Rome, and he in Florence ; so we need not quarrel about him. Yes ! Signor Minuti, I daresay he is far better than I am—he could not well be worse."

" No ! silly child, you are a good girl, and I love you dearly ; and in any trouble mind you come to me, for I have adopted you as my daughter. But then, you see, I have also adopted Alessio as my son—and my children should love each other—or, at least, respect," he added.

"And I will respect him! *You* would not care for him, if he were unworthy. In this world we cannot know each other's hearts, and must be guided by external circumstances; but we can, at least, be charitable, and I fear I have been growing uncharitable. *My brother* is more religious than I, and, therefore, he rebuked me; but I will respect him—and try to believe."

"You are a good child, Ina, and one cannot expect you to forget your trouble; but I can see that you will, in time, conquer it. You have a brave heart, and Providence always helps those who help themselves!"

CHAPTER VII.

PARTING.

ALESSIO saw Ina once again, two days after their meeting on the Colli. She was walking in the town at the time. She spoke to him, and he walked along by her side the length of a street.

"I hope you will succeed well in both painting and poetry! I daresay Signor Minuti will tell me about you; for he intends writing to me." She spoke in a gracious, condescending way, and he replied as a minstrel or troubadour of old might have done.

"Yes, Signorina, I will strive to be great—both because it is well to do one's best, and because I would that you should hear good of me. Your kind wishes will give me strength, your sympathy will endow me with patience."

Ina thought his words a little too strong, and far more than the position warranted. She did not know the man; therefore, she misunderstood him.

"I do not see that my approbation need give you so much pleasure. I am no judge of art. Signor Minuti is both your best friend and best critic, I should say."

"Oh, Signorina, it is your encouragement that is of the most consequence to me. What Beatrice was to Dante, you are to me. There is no one in the world I admire so much."

Ina drew herself up, pride and indignation in her expression. Without a word she left him. And thus they parted.

"She is so proud that she would not even let me admire her," thought poor Alessio, bitterly. His admiration had been so simple and innocent that he could not understand how he had offended. It was such respect and homage as he would have accorded to a queen. He had hoped nothing, fancied nothing, and the mere thought of love, in the ordinary sense of the term, would have been offensive to him. Suddenly, however, an idea flashed across his mind—that she

had not taken his words as they were meant.
What was in reality innocent homage, she
had, perhaps, considered impertinent com-
pliments and love-making. His cheeks
flushed, and his heart seemed almost to
cease beating, so overwhelming was the idea.
Thus Ina herself, was the first to cause the
idea of love to enter Alessio's mind. He
had never imagined that he could dare to
love her in any other way than as a faithful
servant. He now perceived that his words
must have sounded bold, and he also saw
how hopeless would have been any attempt
to court her. She was so proud, so—but
the very thought that he *could* have courted
her, was rapture. Thus he went home
hopeless, but triumphant. She was his
queen—though he could never be her king.

As for Ina, she hurried along, feeling very
indignant. It was not *pride* that had made
her so angry with Alessio; but she thought
that he, knowing her recent disappointment,
should not have dared to speak words of love
or admiration to her. What had she to do
with love? Ah! all men were alike bad—
and Signor Minuti was deceived in his fine
young genius.

But, before Ina reached her home, she was fated to meet with another adventure. She saw her false lover standing by her side, and heard him speaking words of eager pleading. He really was in love with her, after his own fashion ; and, what he could not get easily, always acquired an additional value in his eyes—and he also regretted the loss of her fortune.

"Ina, my beautiful one, look at me! I am dying for your sake! I cannot exist without you."

She turned very pale, but replied firmly, and with irony in her tone.

"I am sorry to hear you cannot exist without me; for, if so, you will die early to-morrow morning, as I then leave Florence for ever."

"Oh, my love, you mock me! Is your heart of stone?"

"Alas, no! it would have been better for me if it had been."

"But you look ill, you too have suffered! I am sure you do love me still! Say you forgive me, and all shall yet be well!"

"I do not love you in the slightest degree,

and it is as much as I can do, to prevent myself from hating you."

"You do not mean that?"

"I do!"

"Oh! you drive me desperate! I shall
commit suicide."

"I do not think you will; but that is your
own affair—I cannot prevent you."

"Cruel one! my death will be at your
door!" and he rushed away, looking quite
tragic.

Conte Carlo actually went to the Lung-
Arno and gazed down at the water; but it
looked so cold and muddy that he turned
away with a shudder, and, going into a
café, ordered some brandy, which he drank
with great gusto. He decided against
suicide, and began to arrange his plans for
finding another heiress.

Ina went into her house wearily. She
was not pained by Carlo now; but she was
thoroughly disgusted. How could she ever
have cared for him! All the world was
hollow and bad, she thought.

She stood by her window that evening,
looking down at the old archway for the last
time. Tears rose in her eyes as she thought

how she had loved the place and all her surroundings. It was here that she had once been happy, and dreamed sweet dreams—never to be dreamed again. The evening light streamed softly through the old arch—the city bells were ringing the hour—and everything seemed sad and subdued, as Ina stood there saying to Florence her last good-bye. In the street below she heard a poor idiot singing a sad and plaintive air in a minor key, composed by himself. This lad's history was a very sad one. When a child he had had a bad attack of scarlet fever, and whilst still in a weakened state his brutal father had beaten him until he had beaten all the sense out of him. Before the man died he bitterly repented his cruelty, and left his only child (the idiot) heir to all his savings, including much jewelry, linen, and a shop. His foolish mother wished to marry their shopman, who loved some one else, but would have married the elderly widow for her money. Had this marriage taken place, and had his two uncles not been left his guardians, the poor Lello would have fared badly. People said his mother was fond of him; but this seemed more than doubtful, for she used to beat her son frequently. And when death seized her—before she had time to commit her matrimonial imprudence —her son's mental and bodily condition was much bettered; although his uncle and nine cousins soon squandered his patrimony. But as they clothed and fed him well, the rest mattered not to him.

At the present time, Lello's mother was still living. He was a stumpy, thick-set youth of eighteen, with a decided taste for music, He would stand still, and listen in silent delight in Ina's garden, when he heard her singing in the drawing-room—for the servants often employed him on small jobs, such as watering the flowers, and carrying the things home from market. One day Ina gave him a cake, and he afterwards said to the servants, with great elation: "The Signorina likes me ; she gave me a cake!" He was simple-hearted, grateful, and harmless. But, unfortunately, he sang in the streets, thereby attracting the attention of evilly-disposed men and boys, who made sport of him. Once they tied him, head downwards, under the arch of a bridge near Fiesole. On several occasions these wretches had nearly killed him by giving him spirits mixed with petroleum to drink—besides exercising their ingenuity in smaller cruelties, such as shaving his head, and stealing his hat. He often said he wished he were dead like his father, and as he walked along the street he sang this sad refrain :—

> " Poor Lello, thy mother has struck thee.
> Poor Lello, poor Lello.
> The mother strikes Lello.
> Poor Lello, poor Lello."

The words and music were his own, and so often did he sing this monotonous, plaintive strain, that others caught it up, and it became one of the popular street airs. Ina often heard passers-by singing " Povero Lello." Lello is now a well-known character in Florence, and is liked and pitied by all but a few street rascals. There was a rough inequality in his voice, as in his poor injured brain—and Ina thought that she had never heard anything more sadly pathetic than that unfortunate lad singing to himself, and calling himself " poor Lello."

Her eyes filled with tears, and she reflected how ungrateful we all are for the blessings we possess. "What if I had been like poor Lello!" she thought.

The shades of night descended, and the stars twinkled above, and Ina said good-bye to Florence. She prayed that if ever it were her lot to return, that she might then have become better, happier, and more resigned.

CHAPTER VIII.

ALESSIO'S IDEAL.

IT was exactly one year since Ina left
Florence, and it was again the early
winter season. Many changes had occurred
for Alessio. He had consented to share
Signor Minuti's studio, and had now become
a professional artist. The old painter had
also persuaded Alessio to live with him, as
he said it was more convenient to be near
the studio. For that reason the young man
had yielded. But Signor Minuti's true
motive was, that he knew the young man
would never rise whilst he continued to live
in the shop—patrons would scorn his surroundings, and he would never enter that
society in which he was so fitted to shine.
The old man would not have encouraged
unfilial conduct, but he saw that a tem-

porary separation was best for all parties. Assunta acquiesced most unselfishly in this arrangement; and, as her son visited her daily, she did not repine. La Fortunata was pleased that her nephew was now a " great painter "—and a gentleman. A distant cousin kept the shop and lived with them, and, as he was completely under Fortunata's thumb, she now ruled the household.

Alessio was a rising man, for Signor Minuti's introduction had made him known, and his own talents had won him appreciation. He was considered a genius, and more than a mere gentleman. The doors of the noblest houses in Florence were thrown open to him, and he never caused his patrons to regret their friendliness. He was a *perfect gentleman*, they said, and his voice and poetic mode of speech were most charming. He touched many ladies' hands now, and many smiled upon him; and yet, so modest was he, and so true, that his queen seemed just as far removed from him as ever.

He heard Ina's letters to Signor Minuti, and though she never mentioned him, he knew that his old friend ever wrote to her in his praise, and often sent newspapers telling of his pictures. After hearing these letters of Ina's, he worked with renewed spirit and vigour. He was now engaged on a large historical painting, and Signor Minuti was touching up a portrait and gossiping blithely the while.

" So Colomba has a little boy, and you are the godfather, and it is called after you ? "

" Oh, yes ! and it is truly a fine child."

" A curious people are your Contadini. Now, when I was up at San Marcello this summer, I noticed come curious facts."

" But you say this to *me*, am I not a Contadino ? "

" Ché ! You never were one—why, you were educated mostly in Venice, and now you are a gentleman."

" You really think so? Am I equal to any other gentleman ? "

" Better, in the essentials, and quite equal in outward polish. But, to continue—one day I went to a mountain Festa, and was entertained by the priest of the place on wine, biscuits, and bon-bons; and I was introduced to all the curates of the mountains. One little man, who had truly need

of a bath, looked so odd, and spoke so well,
that I asked for information about him.
Our host replied, 'He is the most learned
man on the mountains; but he has one
defect.' 'Per bacco! what defect?' said I.
'Well, he is out of his mind. Did you not
notice that he refused to touch the wine
and biscuits? He sees poison in everything, and is in dread of his life.' It never
occurred to any one that the poor devil
should be put in safe keeping and douched
per force. Is not that anecdote curious,
Alessio mio?"

"Yes," he returned, absently; but then,
rousing himself, he added, "other people
are curious, too, certainly that American
was; I mean the one who came to-day and
asked you—'is the Fizzy-ole worth going
to?'—he *meant* Fiesole, but you did not
understand him for a long time."

"That was merely a mis-pronunciation,
and not a national quaintness. Do not think
that I am abusing the Contadini—far from
it; I delight in their freshness and vivacity.
And I know of other lovers as true as your
Bertoldo. When I was at San Marcello, a
case of that kind was brought under my

notice. This is the story. A young girl
had been left in destitution by her father's
death, and her lover, on hearing of the fact,
wrote to her from Sardinia, begging her to
become his wife, and offering to return home
at once if she consented. The answer being
gracious, he did return, and set up house,
provided her outfit, and the marriage came
off in great style. I bought the bride a
present, and they were so grateful that they
invited me to the wedding, and asked leave
to call on me afterwards. But what is the
matter with you, my son? You are not
listening to me;" and the old painter patted
Alessio affectionately on the shoulder.

"Nothing, my father!" replied Alessio,
smiling.

But Signor Minuti was uneasy, and he
walked round the room fidgetting with the
different things. At length, in a corner, he
discovered a painting with its face to the
wall. Turning it round, he looked at it in
amazed admiration.

It was a beautiful woman, dressed in float-
ing white drapery, with a silvery white wreath
on her head, a palm branch in one hand and
a laurel wreath in the other, the glow of a

golden sunset forming a dazzling background, and seeming to encircle her with a heavenly glory.

Signor Minuti uttered an exclamation of wondering delight. Alessio turned, and, observing him, blushed crimson.

"It is yours, of course? Why did you conceal it from me? Is it a saint or an angel?"

"Yes, it is mine. I painted it when alone; I did not leave it here intentionally. I call it *my ideal.* The laurel wreath is to be my crown, and *she* is to give it. The gold is the light of love coming from Heaven and glorifying my ideal."

"Your ideal has a mortal form."

Alessio looked confused, but said, bravely, "Yes! she *has* a mortal form, and an immortal soul. Her spirit is more pure and lovely than anything *my* imagination could create. Surely, it is better to have *her* for an ideal than any beautiful fancy."

"Ah! Alessio mio, as we say in English, thou hast gone ' out of the frying-pan into the fire.' Were you not wiser in loving that little coquette than this proud lady, whom you can never hope to win? Why, she will

not even mention your name. I am quite
out of patience with her.''

" I do not hope to wed her. Surely, it is
as though I loved 'some bright particular
star '—as Shakespeare says—.

> ' What power is it which mounts my love so high,
> That makes me see, and cannot feed mine eye ?
>
>   *   *   *   *
>
> What hath been cannot be.' ''

" Why, cielo ! thou hast learnt English ! ''

" Yes ! It is a most beautiful language,
and I have studied it all this year. I have
already read much of the literature.''

" Ah ! boy, is it not *her* language ? ''

" Yes, it is hers ! Ah ! Signore, do not
laugh at me. My love may seem a madness
to you, but it is great, and real, and all-pervading. My fancy for Colomba filled my
mind and blinded me to the world around
—her image shut out all else—it was a
delusion, a mirage, an unreal love, without
foundation, built of clouds. My love for my
queen is true, founded on admiration, respect,
and all the noble virtues. Witness the effect
upon me. Instead of blinding me to the
beauties of the world, at last my eyes are

truly opened. I never lived till now! I never knew the beauty of the world before. Everything grows brighter and purer—for *she* is associated with all. And, as your Burns says :—

> ' I see her in the dewy flowers,
>   I see her sweet and fair :
> I hear her in the tunefu' birds,
>   I hear her charm the air :
> There's not a bonnie flower that springs
>   By fountain, shaw, or green ;
> There's not a bonnie bird that sings,
>   But minds me o' my Jean.'

She is my all-pervading idea, I cannot think a thought but she is in it. She is *a part of myself*—the better part. She inspires me to noble deeds, to work hard to win the laurel crown for love of her. Oh! Signore, what a blessing is true love ! "

" It has, indeed, proved one to you," said the painter, warmly—" you have grown nobler than ever. But I cannot bear to think that your love will be wasted. Ina will never care for you."

" Love is never wasted."

" But, surely, you look forward to some end ? Do you not hope to marry her ? "

" I have never hoped for such a thing ; she is too far above me."

" Nonsense ! I know grander ladies who would be glad enough to have you."

" I care not for her birth or her wealth ; it is her beautiful spirit that is above mine. I am but worthy to be her servant."

The old painter was almost irritated by Alessio's ideal passion. He thought the young man far too modest ; and that if he could not have Ina he had better turn his thoughts elsewhere. But, after all, perhaps Art gained by this romantic " Aslauga's knight " sort of worship. A visible lady-love might have stayed the painter's hand ; an invisible queen added power to it.

" Oh, Signore, do not think me mad ! I am blessed, most blessed to have known her, to have loved her. I can live content, work content, with the thought of her in my heart. And I know if we never meet again in life that we shall meet in Paradise—and there her heart will understand mine, at last."

CHAPTER IX.

"I ATTEMPT FROM LOVE'S SICKNESS TO FLY."

WHEN Alessio had spoken thus to Signor Minuti, he but told him what he really felt. But, as time went on, things began to wear a different aspect to him. For months Signor Minuti's last letter to Ina had remained unanswered. Anxious, hope-less, hearing nothing of his queen, Alessio began to pine for the visible presence of his love. He found that the ideal was not sufficient—he must see her again at all costs. He grew pale, and thin, and listless.

The old painter watched Alessio anxiously; he saw that he must be aroused from this condition of hopeless melancholy, though disappointment might await him; anything was better than despair. So, one day towards the middle of March, the old man said kindly:

"Alessio mio, I think thou needest a change. Thou hadst better go to the Villa Belvedere at Castellamare di Stabia."

Alessio's face brightened. " Oh, Signore, you are indeed my father! My heart is longing to go—I have felt it dying within me; but I did not like to speak."

Signor Minuti had suggested the last place from which Ina had written, as he thought that Alessio might trace her from there.

A few days later, Alessio had started for Castellamare. Already he felt like another man. A certain energy and determination pervaded his every movement.

He went straight through to Castellamare, spending one night in the train, and arriving at Rome in the morning. He only stopped a few hours at the station, and then went on again.

He was much struck by the aqueducts of the Appian way, the old rows of arches, and the curious tombs and columns—they all seemed to be jostling one another. After that, he did not take much note of the scenery until he neared Naples, and there, the Camposanto, and, above all, the first peep of Vesuvius, were most interesting.

Vesuvius looked a calm, violet-coloured mountain, with a white cloud resting on its top. Who could ever have imagined that hidden fires dwelt within its heart—and that the light cloud was in reality the smoke of the treacherous volcano! At the Naples station Alessio only stopped a short time, and then went on again. How delightful were the fresh sea breezes that blew in from the gulf, by the side of which the train passed. The water was a pale grey; for evening was now approaching. Alessio felt that he was at last nearing his love, and that gave him spirit and courage; and he delighted in all these new sights and scenes. He saw evidences of past eruptions in several villages through which they went; and all the stones and rocks showed signs of a volcanic origin.

At last, he had actually reached the station of Castellamare di Stabia (so called, after the old town of Stabia, that was destroyed first by an earthquake, and then by showers of ashes from Vesuvius). He stepped into a very uncomfortable, jolting carozzella, and was driven to the Villa Belvedere. Truly, it deserves the name of "Beautiful

Sight." But that evening it was too dark for Alessio to observe much. He saw that Castellamare itself was a dirty, low-lying, picturesque village. And he went for some distance along a level road, and then up a steep hill, to what appeared a castellated fortress. Old, picturesque, romantic, he was delighted with his future abode ; and he felt that this was indeed the place in which he would like to meet Ina. They would actually be living in the same house.

On a stone-walled terrace that went round the castle, the carriage stopped, and Alessio noticed how many curious entrances and terraces this castle *pension* had. One of the English ladies who kept the house met him most kindly, but said she had only one small room vacant. It was rather shut out from the rest of the house; but Alessio expressed himself as perfectly satisfied. In front of his window was a fine view of Vesuvius, surrounded by those plains on which are Herculaneum, Pompeii, and the other doomed villages. The hostess told Alessio that the pensionnaires were at dinner in the salle-à-manger ; so he at once proceeded there. With a glad heart he opened the door; for he hoped to see Ina again.

The dining-room was an enormous long-shaped room, with such a length of table that you could hardly distinguish the people at one end whilst seated at the other. Alessio took his place near the head, next to the principal English mistress of the house. Her sister was at the foot of the table, and the French lady partner at one of the sides. Alessio saw that about fifty persons were seated at the table, and he knew at once, by a sort of occult sympathy, that *Ina was not there.* His heart felt a cold chill of disappointment, and he only played with his food—hardly hearing what the kind Miss B. was saying to him.

After a time he turned to her, and said, timidly :—

" Have you not a Mrs. Hume staying here ? "

The lady thought for a moment—" You mean a lady called Hume with a handsome niece, Miss Laurence ? "

" Yes ; are they here ? "

" No ; they were here, but they left two months ago. I have not their address. Mrs.

Hume had been ill, and I fancy she went away for quiet, and that they left no address, because they did not wish any of the acquaintances they had made here, to visit them. My private opinion is, that they are somewhere in the neighbourhood, although they have not been seen by any one. But Mrs. Hume was not equal to a long journey, I am sure. If they are friends of yours, I daresay that by a little patient search you will easily come upon their traces."

"Thank you, Signora."

Poor Alessio! he felt so dispirited that he went straight to his room after dinner, and did not join the others in the drawing-room all the evening.

Opening his window Alessio looked out at Vesuvius. There was no longer the innocent little white cloud over it—it was flaming away now. He had been told that it was only a reflection on the smoke; but Alessio could hardly credit that.

His troubled mind affected him even in sleep, causing him to dream bad dreams. He fancied that he saw Ina on the edge of the inner cone of Vesuvius, and that she fell in as he approached her. He followed her

into an abyss of flame, and stretched out
his arms to save her. But the fire came
between, and he felt suffocated. With a cry
of horror, he awoke—and found that the
morning sun was shining in at the window.

He arose and dressed. Opening his door,
he found himself in a little terrace-entry
with an open arched window looking out on
the yard below. The elder Miss B. had a
room opposite his, and a glass door shut
them off from the rest of the house. This
terrace was full of pots of lovely wild ferns,
and the view from it was nearly the same as
from his room. He saw a distant line of
sparkling blue—Mount Vesuvius and Monte
Somma, with their heads covered with soft
white clouds, and the plains bathed in a
misty morning light. It was a beautiful
scene, and Alessio's artist-soul was cheered
and re-invigorated. He began to hope again.

Going up to the first floor, Alessio walked
through the billiard-room into the garden,
which was built in terraces. A lemon-tree
growing in the garden was covered with
yellow lemons; the gulf sparkled blue and
bright, and the prospect before him was
most beautiful. He was now in front of the

house. He walked down the garden and
stood still, admiring the grand Monte San
Angelo range of mountains, which were so
rugged and picturesque. On every side of
the Villa Belvedere there was a different
view, and each view was beautiful and
interesting. Alessio entered the gardener's
house, which was open to all comers, and he
was delighted by its picturesque interior. A
mild-faced cow and pretty calf, the kitchen
apparatus, and baby's cradle,—all grouped
together in one large barn-like room ! And
then, the dark-complexioned gardener and
his wife, picturesque and handsome, and
their shy gipsies of children, were all alike
interesting to an artist. Alessio thought he
could find plenty of subjects for pictures
here. But, alas ! what would it all be worth
without Ina's presence. He would have
heart for nothing.

After breakfast he set off walking to
Pompeii. He wished to see it, and he had a
faint hope of meeting Ina there. He walked
along a dusty, ill-made road, and saw the
purple San Angelo mountains behind him,
and the brilliant green rice-fields on either
side. At last he reached Pompeii. With

solemn and sad feelings he entered the " City
of the Dead."

He first visited the small Museo that con-
tains casts of the poor bodies, made by
pouring hot plaster of Paris into the moulds
the figures had formed in the warm ashes;
the bones being arranged inside the casts.
They looked so very real and pitiful, that
Alessio went forth saddened.

As he walked over the city he was
astonished by its size, and perceived that he
could not visit it all in one day. He went
alone, and into many hidden nooks where
tourists never penetrate ; for they generally
proceed only by a certain limited route where
the guides lead them. And then they go
away fancying they have seen the whole of
Pompeii ! In the Via Marina, that leads
straight to the Forum, he admired the
beautiful view of old columns and red walls
standing out against the blue hills, with
green ivy growing over the ruins. In one
house (number 10), he saw a young lady
copying the fresco of Romulus and Remus
being suckled by the wolf. Something in
this girl's figure reminded him of Ina. But
on a nearer approach he perceived his

mistake. There was an older lady with her, but she was not the least like Mrs. Hume. Alessio met these two again, and noticed that they were walking alone, which was a most unusual thing in Pompeii, as the guides generally keep with the tourists on week-days, vainly trying to prevent them from chipping the pavements and frescoes to carry away as spoil. Alessio noticed that all the guides who passed these two ladies touched their hats. And, on questioning one of the men, he heard that the elder lady was studying Pompeii to write a book and give lectures on the subject. He found the guides very polite and intelligent, though they considered him a *foreigner*. The reason of this was, on account of the great difference between the Tuscan and Neapolitan dialects. However, they told him that they could understand *him* very well, and laughed good-naturedly with him over the eccentric language of the English and American visitors. Alessio tried to keep out of the way of those tourists who walked the streets of Pompeii talking and laughing loudly; and flourishing their red flags, as he mentally styled their guide-books. In spite of his caution, he did meet one vulgar English couple. The lady walked in front with a gentlemanly guide who spoke English. She must have greatly astonished him when she said :—

"I have no doubt that all these old things have been *put* here."

And Alessio saw her husband slily walking along behind, with his pocket-handkerchief full of stealings.

He then went to the newer excavations, and watched the men digging. With a sad and heavy heart, he was walking towards the place of egress, when he again encountered the guide who spoke English.

"Does not this city remind you of what Dante says, Signor?" asked the guide, and he quoted :—

> "Per me si va nella città dolente,
> Per me si va nell' eterno dolore,
> Per me si va tra perduta gente.
> Giustizia mosse il mio altò fattore :
> Fecemi la divina potestate,
> La somma sapienza e il primo amore
> Dinanzi a me non fur cose create,
> Se non eterne, ed io eterno duro :
> Lasciate ogni speranza, voi che entrate."

" Yes, thou art right. But, tell me, do you live here ? "

" I live here always."

"Is it not very sad, very dull ? "

" It might be to one who could not think. But to one who can appreciate the beauties of nature, it is a most interesting place. When I arise iu the early morning, I go forth and see the sunlight gilding these desolate ruins, and I then think of all the people who once lived in them—and Pompeii becomes to me a library of romances. And then, I sit me down and repeat Tasso and Petrarch, and I feel around me a classical atmosphere—and my heart rejoices in visions of Paradise, where the souls of those poor unfortunates now rest in peace."

"Ah! You have much to think of, friend. I should myself like to stay here for a time, but I fear it would make me too sad."

" Ah, Signore, but we have our comedy as well! The tourists that come in thousands are often so ridiculous, so ignorant, that they make me laugh within myself. But I am glad that they are not here all the time, for they take away all the poetry and romance."

" You say this to me! Am I not a tourist also ? "

" It may be that you are in *name*, but you are quite unlike most of the others."

" And you must be unlike the other guides ! "

" I do not know that! Many of us are well educated; but perhaps I can best explain my feelings. Do you ever write poetry ? "

" Yes."

" Will you not write a poem on Pompeii ?"

" No ! It is too sad, too real; the signs of life are too vivid—it is a *live* ruin to me, and I could not depict it in poetry. Perhaps if I saw it with the morning sun touching it with a light and tender glow, I might then be inspired; but, as it is, I cannot write of it. *You* should do so yourself, friend."

" I cannot ! I feel it too much."

" Ah ! you are a poet also. Let me press your hand."

" Signore, it rejoices me to meet so good a friend. Do you also speak English ? I learnt it from a clergyman in Naples, and I have

read many romances. That English young
lady you saw sketching seems to me like
Rowena ;—I told her—' I have read " Ivan-
hoe," or, as you call it, Ivan-ò ; you might be
Rowena and this dog Fangs.' I had much
discourse with her about poetry, and I sang
her some of the song 'La Bella Napoli.' I had
told the other lady that we would take care
of Mees—and, in fact, we did. She is a most
amiable young lady, and not proud. I shall
never forget her, and shall ever remember
the spot where I saw her sketching."

" Diamine ! how well you are educated,
friend."

" Not so badly—in the summer I go to
teach German in a College."

" I must leave now. Addio ! "

" Arivederlà, Signore. I hope to see you
again ! "

" I will come, if I can."

Alessio left Pompeii impressed by the
guide's intelligence, but by no means as
much surprised as the " Fair Rowena " must
have been. He was himself a self-made
man, one who had risen by the force of
native talent.

Outside the gate of Pompeii he got into
a rickety little carozzella, and, seating

himself by the driver, entered into conversation with him. The man proved
loquacious, and Alessio managed to understand his Neapolitan patois.

He told all his family history, and, mentioning some of his children who were dead,
said :—

"Sono in Paradis!" (They are in Paradise.)
A beautiful way of mentioning death that is
common to that part of Italy. Alessio, as a
Tuscan, had never heard the dead spoken
of thus, and he was much pleased.

"See! Signor; there are the Monte San
Angelo Mountains. On the top of the San
Angelo Mount there is a chapel to that Saint,
and every year he had his Festa, and his
statue made a miracle, and we got some
good things. But the brigands were so bad
that we could no more have the Festa, so we
carried the statue to the church in Castellamare, where it now is. It made a miracle
there once—but now it makes no more.
There are no longer brigands now on the
Monte. I will drive you to the church some
day if you desire it."

"I will think of it. But, tell me, what
was the miracle ?"

"Oh! I saw it myself; it was indeed a true miracle. First the statue was white, then it became red like that woman's cloak, then black as my coat; and, next, it began to perspire, and water ran down. And then it became white again as is a pocket-hand-kerchief."

They had now reached the Pension Belvedere, so Alessio paid the driver and got out.

He was glad to visit all these curious and beautiful things, and even derived a certain pleasure from the thought that *she* must have been there too. But his mind was ill at ease, and he could enjoy nothing properly. So he determined to waste no further time in sight-seeing, but to begin his search in earnest.

Two weeks passed by, but Alessio had not as yet come upon a single trace of Ina. He visited all the country-villages and hamlets round about. And he went to all the islands; indeed, to every place he could think of. He gossiped with peasants, followed other English ladies—but all in vain,—he could not find his queen.

The boarders staying in the Pension were

all interested in him. They thought his
broken English very pretty, and his Italian
most poetic. But they could hardly ever
induce him to converse. He went about
looking sad and hopeless. Every day he
grew paler and thinner; and many were the
sympathizing glances cast upon him. A
very good guess at his story had been
arrived at; for they all knew that he was
looking for a young lady. At last, he
seemed inclined to give up in despair, and
to sit in the garden in melancholy brooding
all day long.

A kind American doctor and his wife, took
a great interest in the young man, and tried
their best to cheer and rouse him. One day
the doctor came to him in the garden.

"But, friend, say, have you been from
Salerno to Amalfi? There are many
English people residing at Amalfi."

A gleam of hope arose in the sad, dark
eyes.

"Thank you! I will go." Then despair
again came over him—"But it will be of no
use!"

"At least try, friend; there is never any
harm in trying."

" You are right, Signore. I *will* try—and, please God, shall have good fortune this time."

" I wish it with all my heart! As you Italians say, 'buon viaggio!' "

CHAPTER X.

THE ACCIDENT.

IT was a beautiful sunny April day when Alessio started for Amalfi. He told himself that this should be his last attempt to find Ina—if he failed now, he would start for Florence on the morrow. He must not waste his life and energies in painful and unavailing "hope deferred." But, in spite of his sadness, his artist-soul was stirred by the beauty around him.

The blue Mediterranean glistened and glittered in the sunlight, and all nature seemed to rejoice. The carriage was now driving along the beautiful winding road cut in the cliffs from Salerno to Amalfi— overhanging the water all the way. Alessio poked the coachman with his stick, telling him to stop a few minutes for him to look at the view—and, standing up in the carriage, he gazed around.

The distant hills of the mainland stretched far out into the sea—a pale violet haze, with a range of snow-capped peaks arising behind, and looking most beautifully white against the cloudless sky. The water was a delicate blue, with lines of a darker shade at certain distances. White-sailed boats moved slowly across its surface, like birds brooding on the wave. Two tall yellow rocks—named the Two Brothers—stood in the sea; and Salerno lay nestling in a distant bay. But, the most wonderful thing in the whole landscape, was the colour the water took near the shore in the numerous little coves and bays. It was a deep sea-green, at once so profound, still, and brilliant, that no one who has not seen it, can form any conception of its surpassing loveliness.

The green, the blue, the yellow, the violet, and white—all formed a picture of wonderful harmonies of colour, framed by the golden sun-light. And Alessio gazed, and gazed again; and felt that it was good to be alive.

" They say that this is the most beautiful

drive in Italy, and, per Bacco ! I think they
are right. Our Viale dei Colli is beautiful ;
but this is more than beautiful—it is
perfect ! ''

The other side of the road was overhung
by the tall cliffs which refracted the sun's
rays with intense force. Although it was
April, the heat was already great. Alessio
told the man to drive on, as it was too hot
to remain longer in the sun.

Every now and again, the carriage had
passed through orange and lemon gardens,
the trees laden with golden fruit. But the
green leaves were already shrivelled up, and
the fruit was sheltered and supported by
wooden frames covered with chestnut
boughs. A short curly-haired boy hung on
at the back of the carriage, or ran along by
the side. When he first perceived this boy,
Alessio had been about to send him away by
a vigorous poke from his cane; but the boy
hastened to inform him that he belonged to
the carriage. And so this original young
footman was permitted to ride behind in
state. His hair was very black, and so were
his eyes; his face was brown, his mouth
wide and smiling, and his teeth were

white and regular. His feet were bare, his shirt ragged, and he wore a small red pointed cap. He was, in fact, a true Neapolitan peasant-boy of a picturesque type. He spoke the Neapolitan dialect, which is in general like the ordinary Italian, with the ends of the words clipped off. Alessio knew the secret of the dialect, so he was able to talk to, and understand, the natives tolerably well.

The boy chattered volubly, and sometimes sang. His song was a sort of droning recitative, more like a funeral dirge than a " popular peasant song." This is the way all the Neapolitan contadini sing. The higher orders cultivate music very fairly, and sing with some spirit. But the singing of the people has a most unpleasant sound—utterly unlike that of the Florentines, who often walk round the town at night serenading most musically, singing their popular airs to the accompaniment of a guitar. Many of them have fine voices, a good ear, and a great capacity of expression. Not so the Neapolitans.

Sometimes the young footman slid down from his perch at the back of the carriage and

walked along the dusty road, amusing himself by catching lizards in the crevices of the
rocks. Once he got bitten, and afterwards
revenged himself by throwing stones at the
offending creatures.

Alessio lay back in the carriage in silent
content. He thought—" How I should
enjoy staying here for ever ! It is like the
Garden of Eden. But what would the
Garden of Eden be without an Eve ? " and
he immediately thought of *his Eve*, and then
grew sad again.

They now passed a house built under a
hollow of the overhanging cliff, the rock
covering it like a roof—it looked frightfully
perilous; for it seemed as if a severe storm
might bring down the whole mass of stone
and crush the poor little house to atoms.
On it was written "Catacombi," and the boy,
Vincenzo, told Alessio that it had been a
convent, and was now for sale. Vincenzo
called a woman who was in the garden, and
made her bring Alessio a monster lemon,
about which there was much bargaining,
and Vincenzo and the woman abused
each other vociferously. Vincenzo was also
very jealous if Alessio spoke to the coach-

man, though the two joked each other good-
naturedly.

They now came to a small village, consist-
ing of some four or five houses and a church.
It lay below the road on a level with the sea,
and it seemed as though people must be
truly in great need of building-land to have
chosen such a spot. A small winding path
led down from the road to the beach. They
could not possibly have brought the building
materials by the path — everything must
have been transported there by water. Surrounded by lemon-gardens and with the
glistening sea in front of them, these
villagers are indeed living in an Arcadian
Paradise ; and can well afford to be cut off
from the rest of the world. Alessio was
so much struck by the picturesque beauty
of this hamlet, that he alighted from the
carriage and scrambled down the wild little
pathway, followed by Vincenzo, whose bare
feet jumped over the stones with surprising
agility.

Alessio visited the little church, inspected
the fishing-boat, and looked at the four
cottages that formed the one street. He
then walked towards the lemon-garden, in

front of which stood a large house, rather more pretentious-looking than the others. The front of this house was shaded by an arbour formed by two gigantic lemon-trees, whose branches were trained over a frame. A bench stood under this shade, and the golden lemons hung down illumined by the sun's rays flickering through the leaves.

It made a beautiful picture. Alessio stood still for a few moments and gazed admiringly, but soon turned away with a sigh. *Ina* was not there! His artist-nature could still take pleasure in beauty, but all too soon a sad thought would intrude itself on his mind and spoil the whole. To him Ina was an idea embodied in whatever was beautiful, therefore all beauty reminded him of her. As he re-ascended the path, he endangered his life several times by looking back at the lemon-bowered house, and not attending to his footsteps. He felt a strange, unaccountable attraction towards that little building.

When he was again seated in the carriage, he asked the coachman whether he could lodge in that hamlet if he wished.

"No, indeed, Signor. All those houses are full."

"There is a beautiful Signorina down there," said Vincenzo, with a grin.

"What Signorina?" asked Alessio, eagerly.

"The Signorina Inglese; she lives in the house with the lemon-gardens. She is English, I know for certain, because one understands what she says. One cannot understand the *Americans*, you know. They are quite different to the English. I know them well, and when one of them speaks to the coachman I tell him not to talk to her— 'she is an American, and non capii.' A little time ago five ladies drove to Amalfi, and I rode behind the carriage as usual. Two of these ladies I could understand, for they were English—the others were Americans, and one understood nothing they said. The young English lady said that one of these was English also; but she must have been mistaken. I know well that they were all Americans. The young lady seemed to admire me much, and she asked me to sing and to tell her all about myself! Diamine! but she *was* interested. I told her that my two brothers are sailors, now in America, and that they can talk English and American, and that they have been to England, America, and Cardiff."

Alessio had made several movements expressive of impatience; and as soon as Vincenzo was silent he hastened to say:

"Does the English young lady always live down there, and has she been there a long time?"

"It seems to me that she has been there some months. Do you know that I am eighteen years old. I am sure that you would not have guessed it! That young lady who drove to Amalfi, and of whom I spoke just now, said that she was much astonished I was so old; for, you know, I am short, and appear young. Oh, I think I amused that Signorina well! When we reached Amalfi, I defended her from the beggars. And when we returned to Vietri, before she and her friends entered the other carriage, to drive home, she gave me some money, just after having refused a beggar; for, she said, *he* had done nothing—and when Pietro said, 'Vincenzo has taken care of the ladies?' she said—'Yes.' Oh! I like the English. I may, perhaps, visit England myself some day, after I have served my two years as a soldier."

"Mille Diavoli! Vincenzo mio, but you have a long tongue!" said Alessio, impatiently. "Tell me, ragazetto, do you know nothing more of the young English lady who lives down there?"

"Altrò! I know all about her. She is rich, and beautiful, and good. And she lives with an old lady, who looks very ridiculous—such a curious old one—we call her the mátta! She does not resemble the old English lady who drove with *my* Signorina to Amalfi, *that* was a good lady! She was dressed in black, and seemed well instructed, and understood all I said to her. The mátta dresses herself like stentorello. She is a *ver buffa.*"

Alessio thought over all that Vincenzo had told him about the two ladies. The description seemed to fit both Ina and Mrs. Hume; but he had been so often mistaken that he would not let himself become too sanguine. He determined to drive to Amalfi, and search that place thoroughly first, and then, if he had not already found them, he

would visit that little hamlet on his way
home.

They drove on in silence—through scenes
that were pretty much the same all the way
—until they reached Amalfi.   There the
carriage stopped in the Piazza in front of the
church.   It was immediately surrounded by
nearly all the natives of the place, who, old
and young, commenced to beg.   Even a tiny
baby, who could neither speak nor walk, yet
understood how to stretch forth its little
hand for alms.

All these peasants were, as a rule, remark-
ably plain; there was a good deal of the
Arab in their type—distinguished by wide
nostrils and thick lips.

Alessio searched the village well, but not
a trace of any two English lady visitors could
he find.   And he entered the carriage again
in a very disheartened mood.

The face of Nature had changed now, and
wore a new expression.   Instead of glowing
colours and harmonious contrasts, a pale-
grey landscape was what Alessio saw as he
drove homewards.   The sky was pale grey,
the water a deeper shade of the same colour,
and dark shadows lay on the cliffs above

and below. It was a calm and peaceful
scene, but, compared to past glories, like
a pencil drawing by the side of a brilliant
oil-painting.

" Ah—life is ever thus! Dead is my hope,
dead is the beauty of the sunlight!" And
Alessio sighed.

They had proceeded quietly for a while,
when, suddenly, Alessio perceived a cart
dashing madly towards them. The next
moment, all was noise and confusion—and
then he knew nothing further.

When he came to himself, Alessio found
that he was lying bruised and half-stunned
upon the ground. The carriage, a battered
and broken wreck, was being pulled towards
Vietri by a pair of frightened horses; and
the cart that had caused all the mischief was
dashing on towards Amalfi. Near to Alessio,
lay the boy Vincenzo, and a little further on,
he perceived the body of the prostrate coachman. He tried to rise, but turned giddy
with the attempt. And he was obliged to
seat himself on the ground again. Vincenzo
arose slowly, and felt himself all over,
saying :

"Holy Virgin! then the bones are not

broken! I am not dead! Diamine! but I must go slowly, slowly, lest I should fall in pieces."

" Come here, Vincenzo mio! Thank Heaven, bambino, that you have received no ill!"

" No, Signor, I believe I am not dead yet," and Vincenzo walked to Alessio's side. " But you, Signor? Tell me, have you received any hurt?"

" Yes! I think I have dislocated my ankle. I cannot walk."

" A thousand devils! this is a bad affair! I will go to see to Pietro now."

Vincenzo returned from his errand with abated breath and a pale face.

" Oh, Signor! he is actually dead—the blood is streaming from him. I have fear —I know not what to do!"

" Run, run, Vincenzo, for help. Via! lose no time."

Nothing loth, Vincenzo did run, as fast as his legs could carry him. He ran as though the dead man were pursuing him; and, to his excited fancy, so he was.

As soon as Vincenzo was out of sight, Alessio began to survey the position of

affairs, and, the more he did so, the more
unpleasant it seemed to him. He reclined
on a hard, dusty road, without a trace of
human-kind, or a single sign of habitation
as far as he could see. His ankle gave him
acute pain, and he felt bruised, and sick, and
giddy. The sea was grey and dreary, and
dark shadows were gathering around.

But the greatest horror of all, was the
thought of the dead coachman; for, like a
true Italian, Alessio felt a great repugnance
to the sight of Death. However, he was a
brave and good man, and never let his mere
feelings overrule his sense of duty. He
must see if the man were really dead. He
could not let him bleed to death unaided.
Setting his teeth to keep back any exclamation of pain, Alessio arose and limped resolutely to the side of the prostrate man.

Though he knelt down beside him, he was
at first unable to look at him; for the pain
of walking had made him feel faint. But,
by a strong effort of will, he kept his senses,
and began to examine into the condition of
his fellow-sufferer.

The man appeared dead, and a gaping
wound in his head showed that he must have

died almost instantaneously. The open, glassy eyes, the blood that had flowed from the wound and lay around, the shattered form, all made a horrible and ghastly picture. Alessio had never seen a corpse before, and he shuddered as he looked at this one. Controlling his feelings, he felt the man's pulse and heart; but soon perceived that all efforts to restore him to life would be quite unavailing. The pulse of life, the breath of life, had gone. It was but inanimate clay that he touched—cold clay, ice-cold. Alessio felt that it was impossible to remain in the vicinity of that terrible dead body—so terrible because there was no feeling of love or friendship to conquer physical repugnance. He pitied the man, but this body was not the man so full of life and vigour an hour ago,—this was only a corpse, a terrible unknown presence.

Alessio arose, but his strength suddenly deserted him; and he sank upon the ground near the coachman's body, and lay there like one fascinated—gazing with startled eyes upon the still white face. The shadows around gathered faster, and perhaps it was the fault of their flickering gloom that made

Alessio fancy he saw the dead man move. So vivid was this fancy, that he again arose and walked away for a few paces, and then, with a sudden cry, he fell down, fainting and unconscious.

CHAPTER XI.

THE AWAKENING.

OUT of the valley of the shadow of Death into the Light—*such Light!* Through the darkest hour to the dawn—a glorious dawn! O'er-shadowed by the cloud—at last to find the silver lining!

Thus, Alessio opened his eyes, and saw ——not the face of the terrible corpse, but that of the woman he loved.

She stood in the light, looking like an angel, so fair and calm. Alessio gazed on her wondering; and thought that he must be dead. This was surely Heaven. Oh! what a glad awakening, so peaceful, so natural, and yet full of unspeakable bliss. This was much better than Life! Thus he mused dreamily, as he gazed, with half-closed eyes, upon the face of her he had loved so tenderly.

Suddenly, his dream was shattered, and he knew that he was not dead. He perceived the very earthly and eccentric form of Mrs. Hume, and it showed him that he still lived. Mrs. Hume, poor woman, did not enter into his idea of Paradise.

"I fear, aunt, that he is very much hurt, and that he will not be able to leave us tonight. It is a great pity, but I think we shall be obliged to give him a lodging for this one night. You know, there is no other house near where he could be properly attended to."

"My dear Ina, you talk as though *I* did not wish the poor young man to stay here. I hope I am not so cruel as that! I think they were quite right to bring him, for his sake and for ours. We will nurse him, and that will be an interest."

"Very well, aunt; as you wish."

Ina now approached Alessio with the light in her hand. Bending over him, she recognised him instantly, and started back. Seeing his open eyes, a deep blush dyed her cheeks.

Poor Alessio saw that this recognition gave her no pleasure, and he sighed deeply.

Alas! it was too plain; he was not yet in Paradise. He spoke with pathetic pride and disappointment.

"Send me away at once, Signorina Laurence! I would not give you trouble or be an incommodo to you. I feel myself very ill—I have fever. I am certain to give you much trouble; therefore, send me away, Signorina, at once, if you please!"

Ina's voice trembled, as she answered, softly:

"I shall not send you away, but nurse you instead. I fear you heard what I said to my aunt; for I did not then know who you were, and I dreaded that the excitement of having an injured man here, might hurt my aunt. If there were no other reason for keeping you here, the friend of dear Signor Minuti would always be welcomed by us. Forgive my seeming inhumanity! Say you forgive me!"

She smiled so sweetly as she spoke, that Alessio could hardly prevent himself from expressing his love, and telling her—that he thanked God that he was not dead, since life had become so beautiful now that he had found her. But he knew he must not speak

his thoughts; for that would break the spell,
and she might then fly his presence.

"Signorina, I have nothing to forgive. I
know well, that you have ever a *good* reason
for what you do and say. You must let me
offer you my thanks for your kindness. I
feel myself most fortunate to .be here."

"But you would feel yourself more fortunate, probably, if you were driving along
the road, un-injured. That is natural;
though being here is better than lying out
on the road."

Alessio was silent; but he thought that he
would rather be here with every bone in
his body broken—than wandering about in
hopeless search, with a broken heart. If he
had been told that he must die for those few
moments of bliss, he would have died most
gladly—knowing that his longing had at
last been satisfied. Love is an o'er-master-
ing passion — and "hope deferred," in
absence, is so terrible that no sacrifice would
seem too great a price to pay for one instant
of hope, love, and *certainty.*

"Is not your aunt here also, Signorina?
It seemed to me that I saw her at the door a
minute ago."

"Yes; she went to prepare a room for you, whilst I looked at your hurts. But I have been very inattentive. Tell me, where are your injuries?"

"I think that my ankle is dislocated. And the shock of the fall has shaken my system. I feel fever in my veins. I have a friend, an American doctor, Signor Smith, who is now staying at the Pension Belvedere. When it is convenient to you, it would be well to send for him. Do you not think so, Signorina?"

At this moment Mrs. Hume entered the room. After looking at Alessio, she said—"Do you know my niece? Somehow, I fancy I must have seen you before! Are you English?"

"No, Signora, I am Italian; but I understand English. I am Alessio Valencini, and I was twice in your house in Florence. I believe you saw me there. I am a friend of Signor Giusto Minuti."

"Oh, I understand it now!" and Mrs. Hume looked very pleased. "Ina, send at once to the Pension Belvedere for Doctor Smith, as this gentleman suggested!"

"Certainly, aunt. Here Niccola, help

this gentleman to the spare room. And you, Vincenzo, take Cola's mule and ride to Vietri, and there hire a horse and ride on to the Villa Belvedere to fetch the Signore dottore, who is staying there."

Ina's orders were instantly obeyed—and Alessio next found himself lying in a clean, soft bed, tenderly waited on by an old Italian woman called Christine, and also by Mrs. Hume herself. He soon found out that he was in that very white house he had so much admired. And he knew that it was the instinct of love that had made him feel such a strange attraction towards it. But, though glad thoughts flitted through his mind whilst pain racked his body, he soon lost the power of considering his sensations—all became a troubled whirl, and then — a blessed unconsciousness.

Ina had been reluctant to shelter the wounded stranger, solely on her aunt's account. She was a woman, and tender-hearted, so she could never have been willing to turn a sufferer from her doors. Mrs. Hume was in very bad health, her heart being seriously affected, and the least excitement was dangerous for her. But, as

she had herself expressed a wish to keep
Alessio, Ina could only hope that no harm
would ensue. For her own part, his coming
seemed to her hardly a *pleasant* coincidence.
It reminded her of past suffering—and of
his past presumption. Her one consolation,
lay in the thought, that a sprained ankle was
not a very serious injury, and that he would
leave on the morrow. His visit was a mere
chance, and he would hardly dare to repeat
it, or in any way intrude himself on them.

The next day Doctor Smith arrived, and,
after examining the patient, pronounced it
as his opinion that Alessio had a bad sprain,
and there had been danger of inflammation ;
but that he thought the young man could
bear the drive to Castellamare, and he
would take him away in the carriage with
him.

Ina communicated this intelligence to her
aunt, and was most unpleasantly surprised,
when she found that Mrs. Hume was determined to invite Alessio to stay with them for
a time.

" But, aunt, I thought you wished to
escape the infliction of any society but
mine ? We left the Belvedere on purpose,

and did not even give Miss B. our address."

" I have found that no society but our own is dull ;—and I wish for a change."

" Would you like to return to the Pension ? "

" My dear, there is society, and society ! "

" So I think. And this young man is not fit society for us."

" Not fit ! "

" Why, of course not ! He is only a common man."

" A common man, indeed ! Are you mad, child ? He is actually a genius, and a *famous man.* All my life I have wished to know a genius ; and now that I have the chance, you wish to disappoint me. Ah ! you cannot deceive me—I have heard Signor Minuti's letters, and read the papers,—and I know he is an extraordinary young man. But you are always unkind to me now ! " and the old lady sobbed querulously.

This accusation against Ina was quite unjust ; for the poor girl bore all her aunt's vagaries most patiently. Seeing that she had set her heart on this thing, and that to thwart her might make her ill, Ina gave up her own will, and, disagreeable though she thought it, determined to ask the young man to stay with them. She hoped that he would comport himself respectfully, and not stay too long.

" You may be right, aunt, as to his being a genius. But it was not all pride in me. You know I do not like any young men now! However, as you wish him to stay, he is welcome to stay. Come with me, and ask him ! "

Leaning on her niece's arm, poor Mrs. Hume tottered into the drawing-room. Alessio was lying on the sofa with his foot bandaged, and the doctor standing by his side. His face flushed, and he tried to rise when he saw the ladies.

" Do not get up, Signore ! We have only come to ask you to stay with us for some weeks, and then your foot will be quite well when you leave. The doctor can visit you here, and it will be much better for you not to move at present."

" Certainly," said the shrewd doctor; for he had been watching Alessio's face, and had made a good guess at the truth.

" Thank you a thousand times, Signora ;

you are too good! But "—and he looked at Ina—" I fear to give too much disturbance."

"Far from it," said Ina, gravely; "your society will prove a great benefit to my aunt. She needs a change, and you can tell her of Florence and Signor Minuti."

"Thank you! Then I will stay, at least for a little while." But Alessio sighed as he spoke. *She* seemed so cold towards him, and took care that he should understand that he was invited for Mrs. Hume's sake alone. But, for all that, he could not help staying. To be near *her* was rapture; to see her, hear the sound of her voice, was to him as water to a man dying of thirst on a burning desert. How he loved her! He saw how tender she was to her aunt, and how gentle to all around her—except to *him*, to him alone she was still cold, alas! Whilst he had been away from her, his love had been abstract and elevated; but now, though no less elevated and ideal, it had also acquired a strong element of personal preference. He felt that he wanted her for his own, not merely to be his *queen*—but as his *wife*. Humble-minded though he was, it was natural that the distance between them

should no longer appear insuperable; for a
year and six months he had been living as a
gentleman among gentlemen; ladies had
treated him as a friend and equal; and he
had even perceived that some of them would
willingly have had this friendship take a
warmer tone. Therefore, it was only his
intense admiration for Ina that made him
still feel that there was a gulf between them.
He knew that he could make her happy —
for no one could love her better. And he
would *try* to grow more worthy of her.
Poor Alessio! though he had found his love,
his trouble grew instead of diminishing.
The more ardent his affection became, the
more he longed to win her.

Mrs. Hume treated Alessio as an honoured
guest; and he limped down to meals with
them, and spent his evenings in talking with
Mrs. Hume in the sitting-room. Ina was
cold and quiet, and he rarely addressed her;
but he often spoke for *her* when apparently
talking to her aunt. And she grew to listen
to him, against her will. Mrs. Hume was
clever in her way, and she drew the young
man out, and was perfectly astonished by
the knowledge he displayed. Ina was more

astonished by the beautiful poetical and religious thoughts that he clothed in such eloquent language. And she could not help owning to herself that there was reason for the old painter's liking him, and that his enthusiastic praise had not been undeserved. She said to her aunt one day :—

"I am always forgetting that he is not a gentleman ! "

"Why, my dear, he is the most polished gentleman I ever saw ! And then, how clever he is ! I wish you would be more amiable to him. I wonder he stays with us ; you are so persistently cold."

"He stays for your sake, perhaps. *You* are kind enough ! "

" I am poor company for a clever young man like that. But his heart is as tender as his mind is strong."

" Well, he may be all you say—only, for my own part, I shall be very glad when he goes away ; for I do not wish to have anything more to do with young men."

So marked had been Ina's want of cordiality towards Alessio that Mrs. Hume felt obliged to apologize to him.

"You must forgive my niece if her manners

are sometimes almost impolite. She has no personal dislike to you."

" I do not think I have any cause for complaint. I know that there is an immeasurable distance between us," he said, bitterly.

" I do not see it ! I think you ought to get on particularly well together ; for, though you are much cleverer than Ina, she is quite an intelligent girl."

" That is not what I meant. But I thank you for considering me as an equal. I suppose Miss Laurence dislikes me—I fear that cannot be remedied."

" No, indeed, she does not dislike you ! Why should she ? The truth is, she cannot bear the sight of any young man, because she has had a disappointment."

" Ah ! " and Alessio winced. " Signora," he continued, " I happen to know all the circumstances of the engagement between your niece and that *vagabondo* of a Conte ; but I had hoped that she had forgotten him by this time."

" She does not care for him any more, and she is very cheerful and resigned ; but he has made her dislike all young men. She is kind as an angel to me, but hard as a stone to you. At least, you will always have the satisfaction of knowing that you have been a great comfort to a dying old woman."

" Not dying, Signora ! "

" Ah, yes ! I feel that I cannot live long."

" Do not say that ! Think of the Signorina ! "

" I do think of her, and that makes me sad. Who will care for her when I am gone ? "

" Ah ! Signora, would that I had the right to care for you both ! "

" Surely, you do not mean that you love Ina ? She who is so cold to you ? "

" With all my heart, I love her. I have loved her for more than a year."

" I am very sorry ; for she will never care for you, I fear."

" I know that, but I am still glad to love her. And, indeed, I cannot help it. She is to me as my ideal."

* * * *

Ina continued outwardly cold and distant as ever ; but she was in reality observant of, and interested in, Alessio. As the time drew near when he was to leave them, she felt that she should miss him—that there would be a blank in her life. So angry was she with herself on account of this weakness, that she avoided Alessio more persistently in consequence. The poor fellow became quite desperate, and felt that he could bear such misery no longer. So he told Mrs. Hume that he must leave in a day's time, as his ankle was quite well now. He said this at breakfast—after which meal the two ladies went up into their respective rooms to read some letters that had just arrived from England.

Suddenly, a shrill and piercing scream broke the stillness. Alessio judged by the direction of the sound that it came from the rooms above, and, from the tone, that it was Ina's voice. He stayed not a moment to think; but rushed upstairs, ready to give his life to defend her. But he found that no defence was needed, or possible, for who can fight with *Death?* Death alone was poor Ina's foe.

Alessio entered the bedroom, and there, stretched on the floor, was Mrs. Hume—quite dead. A letter was clasped in her rigid hand; and Ina knelt beside her with a

white, scared face. She turned to Alessio
eagerly.

" Tell me, is she fainting ? "

He knelt down, felt the heart and pulse,
and examined the body carefully. He then
took it up in his strong arms and laid it
gently on the bed. Turning to a frightened
servant who stood in the doorway, he said—
" Go as quickly as possible to Castellamare
for Doctor Smith ! "

" But you do not answer ! " said Ina,
clinging to his arm, and looking piteously
into his face.

" I fear, Signorina, that she is dead. But
I have sent for the doctor that everything
possible may be done."

She gave a wild cry. " Oh ! dear aunt !
dear aunt ! I have lost you. I am now
quite alone in the world." And she knelt
beside the bed, and kissed the cold hands
and face.

Tears stood in Alessio's eyes—but she
was tearless.

" Oh ! what shall I do, where go to find
peace ? Is there no one in the whole world
to help me ? " She spoke wildly, hardly
knowing what she said.

"Signorina, there is always God to comfort you."

"He seems so far away." She arose and stood, pale, agonised, and desperate, beside him. It would have been better if she had cried.

"Oh, no! Signorina, He is not far away!" and Alessio caught her hands in his own, anxious that she should feel the touch of human sympathy—for, so desolate was she, that even a hand she *disliked* might now be welcome. "Truly, Signorina, my heart pities you—and how much more must the good God feel compassion! Your aunt is a blessed angel in Heaven—think of her joy— she suffers no more. And as for you, He will not leave you desolate. He has taken away one who loved you; be sure that He will give you others to love. Try to be brave—to have faith."

She looked into his face in wild appeal; she did not resent his touch; she seemed to trust him.

"Do you believe—oh! say, is she really dead? Shall I never see her again?"

"I believe both in God and Heaven, and that, though your aunt's body is dead, that

her soul lives truly.   You will meet again—
for you loved each other."

"Yes, how she loved me!"   And Ina
tottered and fell against Alessio's shoulder,
weeping passionately.

It was better thus.   He took her in his
arms and carried her tenderly to her own
room, and, laying her on the bed, stood by
her side watching anxiously.   At last he saw
that her tears had ceased, and that her hands
were clasped, and her lips moved slowly.
She was praying.   He knew that he could
safely leave her now.   But, as he turned to
go, he heard her call him back.   She was
looking at him with grateful eyes:

"Thank you!" she said, softly.   "But
for you, I should have gone mad.   You have
been kinder to me than I deserved."

With the truest delicacy, he attempted no
reply, but silently left her.

When the doctor arrived, he said that Mrs.
Hume was dead.   She had been long in
an infirm state of health, and some sudden
shock must have caused her death.   He removed the crumpled letter from her hand;
and, on reading it, discovered in it the cause
of death, as it announced the total loss of

Ina's fortune. The letter had been, most foolishly, directed to the aunt instead of to the niece.

Ina bore the tidings of her future poverty very quietly. But Dr. Smith thought her so ill, that he sent for his good wife to come and help him nurse her. That night she was in a brain fever.

Alessio wrote to Signor Minuti begging him to come at once. But it was long before he received any answer to his letter; and when it came, it was sent from England, where the painter was staying, engaged on important business. He said he would look after Ina's affairs, but that Alessio must look after Ina himself. When she was well enough she must come to him in England, to live with him as his adopted daughter.

For a long time the poor girl's life trembled in the balance; but, at length, she began to recover slowly. Alessio had suffered terribly all this time; if possible, he loved her more than ever. His manly heart yearned over her with protecting tenderness. And he thought with rapture of how she had cried upon his breast.

When he saw her again, she was looking

very pale and fragile; but her smile was gentle, and her manner sweet and tender. All coldness had left her behaviour; it had but been a defensive armour she had worn since her love-disappointment. But now she had cast it away for ever.

She spoke with great enthusiasm of the kindness of Dr. and Mrs. Smith, and said that the latter had become a great friend of hers. She did not tell him how often the good lady had sung his praises, and spoken of his romantic search for her, Ina. After praising the Smiths, she said :

"And *you*, too, have been good to me! You were also kind to my dear aunt, and made her so happy at the last. She liked you very much. I cannot find words to thank you!"

"Do not try."

"Ah! you do not care for thanks or praise, because you are so good. Do you know, it was you who have strengthened my faith twice in the hour of trouble?"

Alessio's face glowed—"And you, Signorina, have strengthened mine. But, you have yet another friend—Signor Minuti."

"Yes! dear old man! I mean to go to

him in England, and stay with him for a short time. But, as all my money is lost, I shall eventually become a governess."

"Oh, Signorina!"

"Work will do me good. Why, you work yourself. Only, of course, your profession is of a higher order."

"But there is a difference between you and me!"

"Yes. I am not half so good or clever," she replied, humbly.

How he longed to take her in his arms, and tell her that she was his ideal, his queen, his all! Poor Alessio's own heart alone knew how hard was the temptation. But he resisted the mad impulse.

Soon after this, Alessio and Ina were seated together in the train, speeding towards Florence. She was to stay there a day or two to rest. Alessio had written to Colomba, asking her to receive Ina. The answer had been a warm invitation from both Colomba and Bertoldo, who said they had ever remembered the Signorina Inglese and Alessio in their prayers.

Alessio suppressed the latter name, when

he read aloud the letter; for he thought Ina might not like the connection it seemed to imply.

How tender and considerate he was towards her, Ina alone knew. And it would need a woman to fully appreciate the delicacy of all the small attentions that he paid her, and the care for her comfort that he showed.

He was a thoroughly unselfish man, and, therefore, never obtruded himself upon her. His heart was full of a proud joy—" *he was able to serve his queen.*" What more could he desire! He had given up the vain hope of ever winning her love; but he would be a faithful squire, and might yet win her regard.

What Ina's thoughts were Alessio knew not. She had long observed and taken note of his character, and she continued to do this still. Surely, she would have been blind indeed had she failed to perceive what a truly noble-minded man he was; and that in him she might well find the fulfilment of her highest ideal. She was very gentle and grateful, but rather shy and reserved in her manners towards him.

At last they arrived at Fiesole, and Alessio left Ina in Colomba's safe-keeping.

As he walked into the town to his mother's house, he said to himself: "Ah! I am blessed ; I have seen her, and I have helped her. I have won her gratitude and esteem. Now I must work on alone, and strive to do my duty. Perhaps in Heaven she will know me, and lay her angel hand in mine, and then my heart will cease to ache—and she will understand how faithfully I have loved her. Ah! my beautiful one, my light, my guide, mayst thou be blessed! For me, *I* am most blessed among men—because I have loved *thee*."

CHAPTER XII.

ALESSIO'S FAMILY.

WHEN Alessio reached his home, it was late in the evening.

The family were all seated together in the small parlour. Alessio had opened the house door with his own key, and, walking quietly to the room, he stood outside peeping through the half-open door. He smiled to himself at what he saw and heard.

La Fortunata was holding forth to a good-natured fat woman, who had a mountain of frizzettes and false plaits on the top of her head—such a coiffure as delights the more vulgar Italian taste. This woman was knitting, as was la Sunta. A little brow-beaten-looking man sat at some distance from them, furtively pulling a thin moustache; he was their cousin.

" I tell thee, oh, wife! that he is a great gentleman now. Yes, truly!" said Fortunata.

The wife (as they always style a married woman) felt slightly piqued by this excessive praise of some one else's relation, so she said hastily :

"Oh! one knows well, Sora Fortunata, that ' to every bird its own nest is beautiful.' But, porco di Bacco! to me it appears ' better to be head of lizard than tail of lion.' And thou knowest ' a golden hammer will not break the gates of Paradise.' "

" Arch-priest! what affair is this! You are quite an idiot. My Alessio is a *great* painter, not a little one. And, as for your husband !—*he* is rather the *tail* of the lizard ; for he is not even a good carpenter."

" If thou wilt continue to insult me, Sora Fortunata, I go !' "

" Chè! Seat thyself; take not offence! There is ' *no gravy* '* in quarrelling !' "

" Oh! I had no wish to quarrel, only thou wert so high-headed ; ' every one knows how to dance when fortune plays.' But, tell

* " Non ch'è sugo."

me, Sora Sunta, if your Signor Figlio is a great gentleman, why does he not marry?"

"Marry!" screamed La Fortunata—"keep us from it! Why should every one tattle of matrimony? I will not say that our Alessio could not marry if he desired; for there are many great ladies in love with him. But it rejoices me to say, that he has too much judgment to marry in haste, for 'those who marry quickly repent slowly.'"

"'Better a chaffinch in hand than a thrush in the bush,'" replied the sposa, sagely.

Alessio thought that he would rather not play the part of eaves-dropper any longer, and he also wished to embrace his mother; so he walked down the passage softly—and then, returning more noisily, entered the room. Every one rose, and nearly every one screamed or squeaked; for he was not expected. La Sunta arose, and, flinging herself into his arms, wept glad tears upon his breast.

"Oh, my son, my son! How it rejoices my heart again to see thee! Long has seemed the time that thou hast been parted from thy mother. Alessio, light of my eyes, joy of my heart!"

"Ah, mother, I also rejoice, again to behold thee. I have been sick and weary, and there was no one to comfort me. Ah! how I longed to lay my head on thy breast, and know that thou wert there to console thy poor Alessio."

"Console! Mammà mia! It is little consolation that thou shouldst need, Signor Nipote! Is not being a grand painter sufficient for thee? And then, to travel at thy ease and see Rome, and the Pope, and Vesuvius— arch-priest! but thou art an extraordinary young man!"

Alessio smiled, as he saluted his aunt. "You know, aunt, there is no sweet without the bitter, and, 'who is content, gains!' I do not pretend to be a saint, and have my days of ill-temper like others."

"No! my son, I cannot believe that! Thou hadst never an ill-temper."

Alessio smiled tenderly upon his mother, and they sat down side-by-side, holding each other's hands. He knew his mother was only a half-educated woman; but he was not the least ashamed of her for that. Nor would he have changed her for any mother in the world. She was a perfectly unselfish and

pure-minded woman; and her son loved,
admired, and respected her. He thought
that he should never have a wife to brighten
his lot, therefore he must treasure his dear
mother all the more. He would return to
live with her; for what good had his grander
surroundings done him? As he thought
this, Sunta was looking at him with tender,
questioning eyes. She did not feel at ease
regarding his health and happiness. She
sighed as she stroked his hand.

The visitor arose; she had been inspecting
Alessio curiously, and was now satisfied that
she could gather no further information
regarding his appearance; and, for the
rest—propriety now demanded her departure.

"A very happy night to thee, Sora Sunta,
and good repose to thee also, Sora Fortunata.
How are you, Signor Valencini? A very
happy night to you; also to you, Signor
Poldo." And the sposa swept from the
room.

Fortunata began preparing the supper;
and Alessio sat down and asked his cousin
Poldo various questions relating to the business of the shop. When the table was laid

they sat down together and began to eat their supper.

Poldo was a timid little man, and he stood in great awe of la Fortunata; but sometimes he did, and said, very bold things from very excess of fear. He now ate a great deal of maccaroni very fast, and, with a piece still hanging from his mouth, said:

"And hast thou never thought of matrimony, cousin? It is a good thing!"

"Accursed toad!" shrieked Fortunata, with such vehemence that poor little Poldo nearly choked himself, and Alessio could not restrain his laughter.

"Oh! you may laugh, nephew! It is a serious affair, matrimony. A 'good thing,' indeed! *He* had better not try it."

"But, aunt, it appears to me, that cousin Poldo has no desire to marry. And, surely, if he had, it would not be a bad thing. Because one marriage proves unfortunate, so do not all—'the frock does not make the friar.'"

"Oh! thou ungrateful one! Men are a great trouble—we poor women were born to suffer!"

"The proverb says, 'Look at thyself and

then think of me.' Didst thou never con-
template matrimony thyself, aunt?"

"*I!* I thank you, Signor Nipote; it seems
to me that I must tell you that I have 'all
the months of the year.' I have no faith
in men; they are of no value! Why, on
this very day, I met Agnese Biagi, and she
was saying—'Oh! that I could kill first my
husband and then my mother-in-law!' Think
of the shame of a woman saying that! I
said to her, 'You were a fool, Agnese, to
marry a husband'—and she replied, 'I see it
well, now that it is too late!' And when
those two married, all said 'They are two
souls in one nut!' But thus it is ever, with
the men-folk; women cannot keep themselves too far from them; for, 'give them a
finger, and they take the whole hand.'"

"But, aunt, it is not very polite to say
this to me! I am a man."

"It is the worse for you."

Alessio could not but perceive that
"grapes were sour." His aunt was growing
more bitter in her feelings towards the other
sex; possibly because she perceived that her
faded charms no longer attracted them.
Her dislike to the mere mention of the idea

of matrimony was evidently occasioned by
the fear of Poldo's taking a wife; in which
case he might no longer prove so amenable
to her rule. Poldo was not related to
Fortunata, he being a distant cousin of
Sunta's, and not of her brother, the dead
Valencini. Alessio could not help thinking
that it would be a very good thing if these·
two made a match of it; but he knew that
Poldo would, in that case, become an object
for pity. However, if la Fortunata had
made up her mind to have him, Poldo
would never have the courage to resist.
But she did not appear to admire him,
and spoke of his want of spirit with contempt—although she certainly found his
meekness very convenient. She said of
herself, that, if ever she married, she would
have a lively man full of spirit. And she
sighed in secret over the thought, of a few
worn old letters lying in her drawer. They
began—" Gentile Damigella," and ended
with " vostro gentile amante." The writer
of those letters had been spirited, but false ;
and la Fortunata had never had a lover since
she had lost him, when she was only sixteen.
It was well for her, that she had not married

a lively husband with a tongue and temper of his own; for in that case her household might have proved *a little too lively.*

"What have you done all this time, Alessio? Did you go down the Vesuvius? And did the flames burn? And did you cook an egg? Tell us all about it!"

"I had not time to ascend Vesuvius."

"Not time! Then what did you?"

"I was attending upon English friends part of the time."

"Gentlemen?"

"No, ladies."

Fortunata looked suspicious, and so Alessio hastened to change the subject, by presenting his mother and aunt with some handsome silk scarves, that he had bought for them at Sorrento.

"They are very pretty, and I thank thee, Alessio! But, tell me; I hope thou didst not pay what they asked for them, for, remember, 'do not put a razor in the hands of a madman,' and, take care of thy money; for, 'ended the tune, ended the dance'; or, 'without money man does not sing.' Oh! there are such rogues in the world, that it is a great deal of bargaining we must do.

Why, this very day I went to buy a dress, and the shopman was a cunning black-bird ; but, of course, I only offered him a third of what he asked, which he refused, and said it was what it cost him ; so I told him the dress was faded, and I had seen it cheaper at another shop. He then said—' Well, buy it there ! ' So I walked out of the shop— and, lo! he ran after me, and offered it to me for less than before. After much talking, I bought it for a moderate price, and it was not faded and far cheaper than the one in that other shop. What thieves there are in the world ! But I must say, ' the Devil has slept once for me ! ' "

No one answered la Fortunata, and, as supper was finished, Alessio arose.

" Alessio, my son, I hope thou wilt remain with us ? "

" I will sleep here to-night, mother ; but I must return to Fiesole to-morrow ; for I am making a short visit to Bertoldo and Colomba."

La Fortunata looked at him contemptuously. " Why hast thou a wish to visit Bertoldo and Colomba ? They are not fit company for thee. ' Who goes with the lame one learns

to limp;' and, ' better alone than ill-accom-
panied.' "

" They are not exactly friends of mine,
aunt; but they are good people, and wish
me well."

Oh, Bene! It is not for me to speak; to
try to command thee would be ' to bark at
the moon.' A very happy night, nephew ! "

As Alessio and his mother went together
to the young man's room; they heard poor
Fortunata still grumbling to herself in the
distance.

The good Sunta bustled about the bedroom, putting everything in order; she then
turned to her son, and, placing her arm around
him, looked affectionately into his face.

" My son, I see it ! Thou art not happy."

" Mother, I am not happy."

" I knew it, my Alessio. Tell me, is it
that thou lovest ? "

" Ah, yes ! "

" But thou art noble, and clever, and a
gentleman; there can be no woman who
could resist *thee !* "

Alessio smiled sadly. " Ah ! mother mine,
all women think not as thou thinkest. The
one I love is far too good for me ! "

"I cannot believe it! If she were the Queen herself, I should say that thou hadst better love a servant-girl; for—' too dear is that honey that one licks from thorns!'"

"My thought is different from thine, mother. It seems to me, that it is better to love a star than a fire-fly;—the one you can catch and hold in your hand, but its light soon goes out; but the star shines on bright and steadfast—unapproachable—but lighting our path, filling our souls with light, and leading us to Paradise. My life may be sad in this world, mother; but it makes my heart glad and proud that I am able to say, 'I have loved a queen among women.'"

The poor fellow's voice trembled, for his mother was crying on his breast.

"Oh, my Alessio! my poor son! Is it for this that thou hast become rich and famous! That thy heart should be broken for the love of a woman!"

"Dearest mother, grieve not for me; my heart is not breaking; I am weary, I am sad; but I shall not die for love! I hope that I am too strong to be such a weak fool. And then, mother, I am blest in having thee."

"Dearest! But say—" and she looked

up hopefully; " art sure that she loves thee not—that thou canst not win her ? "

" I am sure that she is not for me ; so great a rapture will never be mine ! "

" Have you asked her ? "

" I have won her respect, mother ; I would not lose it."

" Ah! my son, thou wert ever so romantic, thou art a *true* poet ! And if the lady will not have thee, she is most foolish ; but if thou art mistaken, then I pity her, because she is loved by so modest a man, that he even fears to make her the happiest woman in the world."

"Mother! thou dost not know her! I should like well that thou shouldst see her; but I fear it will never be in this world. We must suffer here, but we have the joy of thinking of the world beyond— of an eternity of peace and love. A most happy night, dear mother ; I pray the good God to bless thee! Believe me, thou hast comforted me. Kiss me again ! Addio."

CHAPTER XIII.

NOT BUILT OF CLOUDS.

THE day after Ina's arrival at Fiesole, she said to Alessio that she should like to revisit her old house, before she left for England. She was not strong enough to go alone, and Alessio knew that Colomba would not be a congenial companion for the sensitive young lady.

Willing to gratify her every wish, though always feeling that there was an immeasurable distance between them, Alessio hardly knew how to act. He never forced himself upon her, but rather avoided her than otherwise; for, now that she was poor and dependent, she must be treated with more respect than ever. But when he could benefit her, Alessio always forgot his timidity, for the reason that he utterly forgot *himself*.

So, he now offered to take her to Florence, and said, that they could drive down in Bertoldo's trap at four o'clock, and return on foot before sunset. Ina gratefully accepted his offer; for there was no longer any false pride in her heart; and, had there been, Alessio's manners could never have grated on her sense of refinement.

Colomba said, " Buon viaggio!" and Bertoldo drove them into the town. They went to the old house at once—and a small douceur obtained for them admission, from the old woman left in charge. Alessio sat down in one of the lower rooms, whilst Ina wandered alone over the house. He waited patiently, though she was gone for some time. He could understand her feelings, for they were kindred spirits. Though born in such different spheres of life, they were truly equals; and, if a shade of superiority did exist, it was on the man's side; for his was the more *creative* genius,—hers more contemplative.

At last, Ina came back to him—and, from the traces of recent emotion on her countenance, Alessio knew how sad that visit had been to her. She was unable to speak,

and he did not address her—merely slipping
a rose from the garden into her hand—for
which he received a silent look of thanks.
It was growing towards evening when they
stepped into the street.

They had reached the Viale Principe
Amadeo, when they were suddenly stopped
by a gentleman standing right in their way
on the pavement. Ina looked at him, and
then uttered a low cry, and she unconsciously
clasped Alessio's arm. He drew her hand
through it, and, turning haughtily to the
gentleman, said, firmly :

" You stop our way, sir ! Move on ! "

The man did not move an inch, but stared
at Ina as though he wished to learn her
features by heart. She looked at him
steadily, calmly, contemptuously.

Yes! it was Carlo himself, but how
changed! Shrunken, bald, hollow-eyed,
with an uncertain gait, and blood-shot eyes ;
not intoxicated, but decidedly the worse for
drink,—he was the picture of a fallen man—
of the deplorable results of dissipation. If
Ina had had any lingering regard for him
(which she most certainly had not), it would
now have fled. She might pity him, but it

would be with that pity which is akin to
contempt, not to *love*. She shuddered as
she thought of what her fate might have
been, linked to such a man.

She turned hastily from him to Alessio,
whose fine manly countenance expressed the
tenderest sympathy for her. Yes! she
could not help clinging to that strong arm,
with a comforting sense of trust and re-
liance. She knew that, come what might,
he would be ever ready to help and protect
her.

"Ina! Miss Laurence! Will you not
speak to me? I have heard nothing of you
all this time, and I have been so anxious.
You look pale ; have you been ill ?"

"Canaccia!" muttered Alessio under his
breath. But, turning to Ina, he said, some-
what stiffly—"Do you wish to speak to this
Signore, or to proceed ?"

"Oh ! go on, please."

And, without one look or word, she turned
from her old lover; who was so much astonished, and felt so crestfallen that he hardly
knew what had happened, when he felt a
strong arm push him aside, and then, saw his
former betrothed passing down the street on

the arm of that "low jeweller." He cursed
them both, and his luck, too, as he slunk
away. There was now no chance of Ina's
guineas repairing his shattered fortunes.
The life of a gambler was the only career
open to him in the future. No other heiress
would be likely to fall in love with him, now
that his manly beauty was lost.

And Alessio! how his heart swelled with
joy and pride, as he walked off with Ina
clinging to *him.* He had feared that Ina
still regretted her old lover ; but he now saw
how little his appearance affected her. She
had been evidently much disgusted by the
appearance of the ruined rake. But he
wisely forbore to speak; for he knew that
she must have been, to a certain extent,
overcome by this revival of old memories.

When they reached the Piazzo Cavour,
near the Porta San Gallo, they perceived a
great crowd and commotion. A runaway
horse was tearing wildly towards them, with
its pale-faced rider clinging to its back.
Quick as thought, Alessio placed Ina on the
path, and, with a hurried pressure of her
hand and a look that revealed all his secret
feelings, he dashed into the road. When

the horse came near him, he seized it by the bridle, resolutely stopping it, and using his great strength to curb the maddened brute. It struck out at him, kicked, and tried to bite. But, at last, perceiving it had met its master, it gave up all resistance, and stood perfectly still, hanging its head and quivering all over—the picture of a cowed and beaten creature. Alessio then gave it in charge to some men, and turned to the dismounted rider, who was thanking him warmly. The crowd set up a shout, and many people insisted on shaking hands with him. When able to free himself from these too-friendly persons, he again rejoined Ina, and noticed that she had turned very pale.

" Were you very much frightened?" he asked, anxiously.

" Yes!" she answered.

" Are you well enough to walk? Do you wish that I should take a fly?"

" No, thank you; I prefer to walk."

They proceeded in silence for some time, and then Alessio began to speak of Colomba. Alessio talked Italian to Ina, as she knew the language thoroughly, and used all the Italian idioms.

"I think she is happy," he said. "She and Bertoldo are contented in their way— they are well-matched, too, neither being the intellectual superior of the other. At first, Colomba said she wished that she had married a richer man; but now that Bertoldo is so prosperous she can delight her heart with jewels and fine clothes. She is also fond of her baby, and has at last become sufficiently serious for a wife. And, if she is sometimes a little too foolish, and Bertoldo rather too passionate, and if he beats her a little—that matters not! They are fond of each other all the same. Their feelings are not refined. They are a pair; 'two souls in one nut.' I am sure I can never thank Colomba enough, for showing me what a silly little flirt she was; for, had she not done so, I might have married her, and found it out afterwards when it was too late. We are now good friends; far better than we should have been if we had married. For, you can well understand, Signorina, that Colomba would have been no companion for me. I——"

Ina had left Alessio's arm, and he now put out his hand to help her as she suddenly stumbled. He drew it back with a sup-

pressed exclamation, and stood still, looking
very pale and troubled. They had reached
the top of the hill that leads to San Domi-
nico; at this point there is a stone bench,
backed by cypress-trees, and a little further
on this footpath joins the new carriage-road.

" What is the matter ? " asked Ina
anxiously.

" Nothing to alarm you, Signorina. I
have only hurt my wrist, and it makes me
feel rather faint."

Ina crossed to the other side of Alessio
and drew his uninjured hand through her
arm. Her touch acted as a restorative, and
he walked with her to the stone bench, where
they seated themselves.

But Ina arose quickly, and, leaving Alessio
there, went through a gap in the hedge into
a neighbouring field, and walked on until
she came to a little stream, in which she
soaked her pocket-handkerchief. Returning
to Alessio, she bound the handkerchief round
his wrist. He had revived, and the colour
was returned to his cheeks and lips.

" What hast thou, Signor Alessio ? " said
Ina, tremulously.

" Thank you a thousand times, Signorina,

for your goodness! Be not alarmed for me;
I have but sprained my wrist—and the water
has done me good already.   It was the
sudden movement that caused me to feel
faint.   I was so stupid as to forget my
sprain.   It is nothing!   Think no more of
it, Signorina.   Had I broken even my arm,
your kindness would have made the pain a
pleasure to me!" he added in a passionately
tender tone.   Then, fearing he had offended
her, he said lightly : " I did not know that I
possessed such delicate nerves.   It appears
to me, that I am becoming a child again!"

" Ah, no! Signor Alessio, *your* nerves are
not delicate.   They are as strong as your
courage.   I am certain that you have sprained
your wrist badly; you must have done it
when you stopped the horse.   I fear it may
be more than a sprain; and that you have
dislocated your wrist!   Oh! why did you
walk back with me!   You should have gone
to a doctor at once.   It was very wrong, very
noble,—very——why did you not tell me of
it?   I—I——"

" I did not tell you, Signorina mia, because I wished to have the pleasure of walking home with you.   And, as for the doctor!

It seems to me to be time enough to think of one, when I have nothing more to do for you."

Ina turned away; and so Alessio could not see the tears that glistened in her eyes—still less could he read the feelings of proud joy and of yearning tenderness that filled her heart, as she thought "*this brave man loves me*," and knew that he counted pain as nothing when borne in her service. He was a true gentleman, a true Christian; and, ah! what a lover to possess!

" It was very brave of you to stop that horse."

" It was only my duty."

" Then it was brave of you *to do your duty.* Every one has not the courage to do his duty."

" I thank Heaven that so much courage is given to me; without it I should be less than a man. Ah! Signorina, you see well that it is for this, that we men have strong nerves and muscles. It is the poor ladies who have to suffer most in this world. Tell me, were you frightened? Did you think the horse would kick you? I saw that your cheeks were pale. But, surely, you knew that *I* would let nothing harm you!"

Ina blushed crimson, as she replied, in a low voice—"Signor Alessio, is it possible, that you really think so badly of me! You might have known that my fears were for your safety alone."

A glad light shone in his eyes, as he said, gently:

"Thank you, Signorina; I am glad that you consider me as your friend—that you care for me a little—that you would have been sorry if I had been killed."

"You are the best friend I have in the world. And you must not say that I should be only '*sorry*' if you were killed." And there was a sound of tears in Ina's voice as she spoke.

Alessio's heart beat madly with hope; but he told himself that she was only *grateful*, and that she spoke so frankly just because she did not consider him as an equal. He thought—"Poor Ina! my beautiful queen! Yes, she is indeed lonely; and I am her only friend, in Italy at least; for Signor Minuti is far away in England. How I long to tell her my love; to convince her that she was made for me and I for her; that we are both sad and lonely apart. Oh! what rapture we might feel if united for ever. But she loves me not—she may never understand me on earth. Yet she trusts me, and that is much. I cannot win her, I must say addio!"

"Yes, Signorina, I am your best friend; for no one on earth can long to serve you, more than I do. Call me your true knight, your servant, one who will be faithful to you even unto death. I will write poems of you, as the Troubadours of old, wrote of their fair queens, and, perhaps, when you are far away; my songs may reach you, and you will think of me with kindness as you read them. And then you will say to yourself—'I am glad that he has become a poet for love of me!' and I—I shall rejoice if you ever think of me; for I live but to love what I can never win."

Ina blushed again; but a glad light shone in her eyes, as she turned them timidly upon his sad face. Her hand stole silently into his, as she said softly :

"Oh, my friend, that will not be my thought—I shall think—I shall think— Ah! Alessio mio! *I love thee.*"

The last words were said so softly, that he could hardly catch them, and she hid her blushing face in her hands as soon as they were spoken.

To Alessio, all the world seemed suddenly filled with light. Love illumined the whole universe. For a moment he was too happy to think; but when he did think, he doubted the evidence of his own ears, and longed to listen again to that tender avowal.

" Signorina Ina," he said, in passionate pleading, "forgive me if I am mad !—but tell me if you said you *loved me ?* For me, I love you better than life itself. Love breaks my heart—fills my soul with light— and is a rapture and an agony. And yet, mine is not mere passion—it is *love,* tender and true. I long to make you happy ; to be your husband, strong to protect you, true to cherish you. I feel that you were made to be my queen, and that I can love you as you deserve to be loved. If I am unworthy —*love* shall raise, ennoble me. Ah ! Bella, I would have been silent—been silent until death stilled my pain, had not those blessed words of yours filled me with a wild hope. I owe all that is good in me to you—you inspire me to paint, to write. Say, Signorina Ina, can you repeat those words ? Will you accept my faithful heart ? Wilt be my wife and queen ? "

He drew down one of her hands, and looked into her face with tender and earnest appeal. Her eyes fell, but not before he had read his answer.

She said but three words, more softly than before—they were only a repetition :

" *I love thee.*"

He clasped her in his arms, and she lay nestling on his breast, crying glad tears of sweet delight.

" Ina, my beloved, thou art mine at last ! "

" Thine for ever, Alessio. Thou callest me thy queen—I say that thou art *my king*. There is no one in the world so good as thou art, and I could not help loving thee, my own. I am all unworthy of thee—not good enough to deserve thy love."

" I should say the same to thee, Cara, so we will not speak of that more. To me, thou art a queen, and I am to be thy king; let it remain so—and thus, we both are blest. My religion is now the same as thine, for I

have become a Protestant. But thou wilt
dislike my relations, Ina mia, perhaps ; for
they are not like thee ? " he added, half
doubtfully.

" Thy people shall be mine, beloved. That
love were little worth that could not love
what *thou* lovest ; that wife but half a wife
who could not become a daughter to the
mother who loves *thee !* "

" I thank God for thee, Ina bella ! " he
replied, tenderly, as he pressed his lips to
hers.

Her head rested on his shoulder, and his
arm was clasped around her. They sat in
silence. Both were perfectly happy—too
glad for speech—and yet, with hearts in such
perfect unison, that they were unaware of
external silence, and felt as though they
spoke. The language of true love rises
above the power of mere words.

Both in their hearts were giving silent
thanks to Heaven for the blessing of their
perfect love.

The sky was a pale olive-green, streaked
with gold, and merging into deeper blue.
The distant hills were a soft lilac—the
dark cypress trees stood out clearly, tall and

stately, against the evening sky. The muffled sound of bells was borne on the quiet air—and all things seemed peaceful and at rest. Still, the lovers sat there silent. At last they arose—and walked on, hand in hand, united in their perfect love for ever.

FINIS.

WYMAN AND SONS, PRINTERS, GREAT QUEEN STREET, LONDON, W.C.

No. 5.　　FLORENCE FROM THE VIALE DEI COLLI.

(*See page* 76.)

No. 6.

VILLA BELVEDERE AND TERRACES.

(*See page* 110.)

No. 7. FIESOLE. *(See page 180.)*